# The Army Doctor's Wedding

Helen Scott Taylor

## Other Books in the Army Doctor's Series

# Acknowledgments

Thanks to Mona Risk, my excellent critique partner, who has been with me through thick and thin since the start, to my son Peter Taylor for his skill creating book covers, and last but not least, to my trusty editor Pam Berehulke for her sharp eye and good commonsense suggestions.

# Chapter One

Alice Conway stumbled across the arid, rocky ground, a precious newborn baby clutched to her chest. The rattle of gunfire sounded behind her, each shot searing along her nerves. The three African women with her held their children in their arms, still running fast. Alice couldn't keep up with them for much longer. Her legs felt so weary, the muscles weak and aching, her feet sore.

She glanced over her shoulder as a rebel jeep crested the hill behind, about two hundred yards back. Pure terror streaked through her. Her little group of survivors was nowhere near the refugee camp yet. She would not get these women and children to safety in time. They would all be mown down in a hail of bullets like the rest of the villagers.

Her breath sawed in and out, so loud in her ears that it took her a few moments to notice the rhythmic beat of a helicopter approaching. She blinked away dust and sweat and realized there were two helicopters coming from the direction of the refugee camp. Were they friendly?

If they were government troops, they were likely to fire on the rebels and cut down the women and children in the crossfire. Neither side fighting over this war-torn country cared about the safety of civilians. If the vulnerable died they were just collateral damage, or worse still they were raped and murdered to spread terror. The charity Alice worked for did its best to help the women and children, but it was like trying to hold back a tide of hatred.

The smaller helicopter drew level. Alice's heart leaped with hope at the NATO logo on the side. The rebel jeeps sped up behind them, bullets thudding into the ground all around. NATO soldiers returned fire. The other helicopter hovered, preparing to land fifty yards ahead.

An almighty bang sounded behind. Heat and dirt blasted in all directions. Spatters of burning fuel showered the area, setting the small dry bushes on fire. One of the jeeps must have exploded. Alice ducked her head and hugged the tiny baby, running faster.

A stab of hot pain jabbed her calf. She stumbled, tried to right herself, but knew she was going down. She threw out an arm to save herself and angled her body to protect the baby.

Poised at the door of the Merlin helicopter, ready to jump out, Maj. Cameron Knight recoiled at the thunderous sound as a shell hit a rebel jeep. With a fiery flash and burst of black smoke it exploded. His gaze jumped back to the women and children. The three native women had cowered, huddling together. He couldn't tell if they were injured, but the blonde woman had gone down.

Cameron shifted his boots on the metal rim of the door, his gaze darting from the ground to the downed woman. His fingers flexed on the strap that held his medical kit on his back, eager to be down there.

"Wait, Major." The voice of the captain in charge of the unit shouted over the noise.

Cameron outranked him but as a doctor his rank was meaningless in combat situations. He was supposed to do what he was told. Nevertheless, he'd learned a long time ago that the British army cut doctors a lot of slack, and he took every inch he could get. He was here to offer front-line medical care, life-saving resuscitation, and damage-control treatment in combat situations. He did what needed to be done even if it was dangerous.

The second the chopper touched down, Cameron leaped out and dashed towards the casualty. She hadn't moved since she fell. If she'd taken a bullet she might be bleeding out. There was no time to waste. With a curse, the captain sent two soldiers out to protect him.

Doctors weren't supposed to be in the line of fire but the fact Cameron didn't carry a gun was irrelevant. He needed to be out here where the wounded were.

He slid to his knees beside the woman, a gun discharging over his head. He tuned out the metallic rattle and concentrated on the patient.

She groaned as he gently rolled her over. Her eyelashes fluttered, revealing blue eyes. "The baby," she whispered, trying to move the arm she had fallen on. She winced in pain and Cameron realized she had a cloth-wrapped bundle inside her jacket. He pushed aside the fabric to reveal the head of a tiny newborn. The infant had a unilateral cleft lip. Something to be checked when they got back to base.

"Major Knight, there are more rebels coming. You need to get the woman in the helicopter," the captain shouted.

Gesturing his acknowledgment, he examined her quickly. Blood covered her lower leg, but it was only a flesh wound. With a bloodied nose and bruised cheek, she'd probably have a couple of black eyes—but it was her arm that worried him most. It lay at a strange angle, almost certainly broken in a couple of places.

The baby's vitals should be checked, but that would have to wait until they were in the helicopter. Not that he could do much for the child if it were distressed. He certainly wasn't a neonatologist, and he didn't have the equipment to treat a newborn.

He signaled to his combat medical technician, who ran over with a stretcher. They lifted the woman on and carried her back to the helicopter.

Cameron tried to take the tightly wrapped baby from her good arm, but she hung on. "No."

"I need to examine him. The baby will be safe. You can still see the little guy."

"Okay." She released the infant.

Cameron unfolded the bright red and yellow fabric from the tiny body, noting the tied-off umbilical cord, which should be dealt with. Tension gripped him while he completed his visual check. The child had not sustained an injury. He released a breath and took the baby's temperature and pulse.

"He seems fine." Cameron settled the boy in a secure pouch beneath a seat. They weren't outfitted with transport cribs.

He turned his attention back to the woman. "I'm Major Knight, a doctor with the British army."

From the few words she'd spoken he thought she had a British accent, but he wasn't certain. He recognized the logo on her jacket, a hand cradling a baby. It was a charity caring for women and children in conflict zones. "What's your name?" he asked gently as the helicopter rose into the air.

"Alice Conway. How are the others?" Raising her head, she tried to see. Cameron glanced over his shoulder to where the medical technician was checking the African women. They squatted in a group, their children tight to their sides. Their suspicious dark eyes fixed on the soldiers distrustfully. It was little wonder considering the way they were used to being treated.

Cameron pressed his lips together with a burst of frustration over how powerless the British army was to really make a difference here. As soon as NATO pulled out, everything would go back to how it was before. But now wasn't the time to say such a thing. He returned his attention to Alice and forced a smile. "They're safe." For now.

Alice relaxed and her eyelids fluttered as she fought to stay awake. "My arm hurts."

"I'm afraid it's broken, but we'll fix you up at the military field hospital."

"My leg burns as well."

"That's nothing to worry about. Just a flesh wound. I'll dress it in a moment. Let's make your arm more comfortable first."

The baby let out a thin, urgent wail. Alice reached out her good arm and touched the tiny bundle. "It's all right, sweetheart. I'm here."

Whether the baby responded to her or it was just coincidence, Cameron didn't know, but the child quieted.

"He must be hungry," Alice said. "He was born about three hours ago and he hasn't been fed yet. I gave him a few drops of water on my finger but that's all I could do." A sigh whispered between her lips and her eyelids fell.

"I'll have him checked over by someone with more experience in pediatrics when we get to the hospital." Cameron stroked the sweaty blonde bangs off her forehead. He had an overwhelming urge to touch her, comfort her.

She shifted her position and a moan slipped between her lips.

"Your arm?"

"Yep."

"I'll give you a shot for the pain and strap it up."

It was so good to be safe, to be lying down with someone taking care of her. The doctor cut away the sleeve of her jacket to expose her arm. He retrieved a small glass ampoule from his pack and held it upside down before jabbing the syringe needle in and drawing out the liquid.

She closed her eyes as he gave her the shot, willing it to take effect. Her arm ached like crazy. Every time she moved, pain shot into her shoulder and down her body. The throb in her head and sting of her lower leg were nothing in comparison.

"We'll give that a few minutes to take effect before we move your arm."

Alice opened her eyes to find the doctor leaning over her. His fingers gently probed the bridge of her nose and beneath her eye.

His eyes were dark brown and gentle. A man who did his job must be kind and compassionate. His gaze moved to hers. A smile curved his lips and crinkled the corners of his eyes. "The good news is there're no bones broken in your face. You'll look like you've gone ten rounds with Mike Tyson, though."

She smiled in response, despite her pain. "What did you say your name was?"

"Major Knight." He leaned a little closer. "As you're a civilian, you can call me Cameron if you like."

Alice reached a hand towards the baby again and stroked the little cloth-wrapped bundle, hoping her touch let the tiny boy know he was safe. Just the thought of what the villagers would have done with him made her eyes tear up. All because the poor little guy had a cleft lip.

Cameron moved to work on her leg. Alice closed her eyes and drifted. She was so exhausted; she struggled to stay awake. She and the women from the village had run for three hours, driven by fear to reach the refugee camp on the outskirts of Rejerrah before the rebels found them.

The sound of the soldiers' voices merged with the

noise of the helicopter engine and the floor vibrated against her back. Strange smells assailed her: the metallic stink of oil, the tang of antiseptic. Something cold rubbed over her leg. It stung, then paper ripped and a soft dressing pressed onto the wound.

Cameron touched her shoulder. "Are you okay, Alice?"

"Just dopey."

"Nothing to worry about. The analgesic has a mild sedative effect. Your leg wound is only minor. I suspect a stone or piece of debris hit you when the jeep exploded."

He pulled a blue sling out of his pack and unfolded the straps. "This is going to hurt a little, but your arm will be more comfortable once we have it supported."

Alice gritted her teeth against the jab of pain as Cameron gently moved her arm, folding the forearm against her chest before securing it in the sling. After fastening it, he touched a hand to her cheek. "There you go. That will keep it still until we reach the field hospital and set it properly."

"Will you do that?"

"I can if you like."

"Yes, please."

Alice didn't like men much. She'd seen enough evidence that they weren't to be trusted. Not just here, in the conflict zone, but back in Britain as well. Yet she did trust Cameron. There was something about him that made her feel safe. Maybe the red cross on his jacket sleeve, or maybe his caring smile, or the way he handled her so gently.

The tension eased from Cameron's shoulders. It looked like there was nothing seriously wrong with Alice. In a few weeks the minor injuries would have healed. By six weeks the broken arm would be mended as well.

Lifting the tiny baby, he settled him in the crook of

Alice's good arm. Despite the ordeal the infant had suffered in its first few hours of life, its pulse was strong and its temperature normal. Some people were survivors and this baby seemed to be one of them.

With a smile, she kissed the baby's head. "You're such a good boy, aren't you, sweetie?"

She seemed very attached to the child considering he was only a few hours old and obviously not hers. How had she come to have him? From what he'd seen, she had fallen hard because she tried to protect the baby. That was why she'd hurt her arm. She'd protected the child at her own expense.

He glanced at the small blonde woman with respect. He did his bit to help the locals if they were sick or injured but he operated under the protection of the military. Charity workers like Alice had no such protection. Their charity status did not always shield them from violence.

"The baby's cleft lip can be repaired, can't it?" she asked, a note of concern in her voice.

Cameron poked his little finger in the child's mouth and explored the soft palate. "I can't feel a gap in the roof of the mouth. If it's only the lip involved, then the surgery is straightforward. You will need a plastic surgeon for it, though."

"ETA five minutes, Major," the captain said.

"Understood."

He fastened straps around Alice to secure her. "Hold the baby tight. We'll take you both in together on the stretcher."

"Where are we landing?" she asked.

"The military base at Rejerrah. You and this little guy will be admitted to the field hospital. I'm afraid the three women and their children will have to go to the refugee camp. At least they will have food and shelter and a measure of protection."

"As long as they're safe." Alice hugged the tiny boy

and settled back on the stretcher as the helicopter landed.

The medical technician took one end of the stretcher and another soldier on the team took the other.

"Ready," Cameron said, touching the back of Alice's uninjured hand.

"Yes. I want to get myself sorted out quickly so I can look after the baby." She gripped Cameron's hand, and he met her determined blue gaze. "You will help me get the best care for him, won't you?"

"Of course."

"Promise?"

Cameron was taken aback. Patients didn't usually question his dedication to the job. Yet he could understand her being concerned for the baby.

"I promise I'll do whatever I can to ensure the little guy gets top-notch treatment."

# Chapter Two

The hollow footsteps of army boots on the cement floor echoed as two soldiers wheeled Alice down a hallway on a gurney. Bundles of cables and pipes ran along the ceiling and harsh neon lights spaced down the corridor lit the way.

The field hospital did not feel welcoming. Alice hugged the baby closer and glanced back to check if Cameron was still with them. Her breath hissed out in relief at the sight of him a few steps behind, writing on a clipboard.

They turned into a room containing a bed, a small table, and a plastic chair. One high window allowed a weak beam of light to filter into the room. The army medical technicians lifted her across to the bed and left with the gurney. A nurse in army uniform came in with Cameron.

"This is Acting Corporal Lane," he said. "She's going to prepare you for surgery." He came closer and moved the fabric away from the baby's face. "How's the little guy doing?"

"He's been wiggling a lot more since we arrived." At that moment the baby let out a mewling cry.

"Sounds hungry to me," Cameron said.

Alice wondered how much experience he had with tiny babies, but now wasn't the time to start asking questions like that.

A pretty redheaded nurse came in, a smile lighting

her face as she set eyes on the baby. "Oh, he's adorable. May I take him?" When Alice nodded, the nurse lifted the infant into her arms and cradled him. "Thank you for paging me, Major. You've made my day."

Cameron moved to the nurse's side and joined her in examining the baby. "As soon as we arrived I thought of you." They shared an intimate look and Alice pinched her lips together. Were they a couple? Surely the army didn't allow officers who served together to date. And what business was it of hers, anyway?

"He's a few hours old and hasn't been fed yet," Cameron said.

"Does he have a name? I'll register him in the system, examine him, and do all that's necessary to make him comfortable."

"His mother died before she named him," Alice said. "His father was called Sami. He died when the rebels attacked the village. Maybe we could name the baby after him?"

The nurse nodded and turned to the door.

"Bring him back when you're done," Alice blurted.

The nurse paused, her questioning gaze jumping from Alice to Cameron.

Cameron simply nodded.

The nurse left. Alice bit her lip, anxious now the baby had been taken. If he ended up being handed back to the locals, she feared for his safety. Because of his disfigurement, his people thought he was cursed and would have left him to die. Granted, the city dwellers probably had different customs than the nomadic people who lived in the desert, but if he was sent to an orphanage, anything could happen to him. She felt personally responsible for the poor little thing as she'd helped bring him into the world.

Cameron's hand settled gently on her good arm. "Lieutenant Grace will take good care of him. She worked as a pediatric nurse before she joined the army, so she has lots of experience with babies." He stepped back with a smile. "I'll leave you in the capable hands of Acting Corporal Lane while I clean up. See you in the OR."

With a confident stride, he headed towards the door. "Thank you, Cameron."

He paused and turned, a smile lighting his face beneath the helmet he still wore. "You're welcome, Alice. See you soon." Then he was gone.

The nurse chatted as she helped Alice take off her shorts and the remains of her jacket, then cut away her T-shirt beneath.

"Let's clean you up, shall we?" She brought a bowl of water and a washcloth and left while Alice soaped herself down using one hand. It had been a couple of days since she had washed and she was aware she probably didn't smell good. She hoped Cameron had been too busy to notice.

Once she was clean and gowned, the nurse helped her back in bed and put an IV in the back of her uninjured hand. "This is for the anesthetic. You won't have to put up with it for long."

Two men in uniform came in and lifted her onto a gurney, then wheeled her along a maze of corridors. They pushed her into a small room where a technician gently lifted her arm out of the sling and took some X-rays. Then they wheeled her to the OR.

Plastic sheeting covered the walls and machines bleeped and hummed. The gowned and masked medical team worked around Alice, attaching monitors and preparing. Relief burst through her when Cameron strode in with a female doctor at his side.

"How do you feel?" He leaned over her, gowned and capped in green scrubs, his mask loose around his neck, and rested a hand on her shoulder.

"Nervous."

"No need to be. This won't take long. When you

wake up your arm will be set in a cast."

The female doctor stepped up beside him. "Hello, Alice. I've heard a lot about you." Dark curls peeped out from beneath the green cap topping the woman's heart-shaped face. She smiled and instantly put Alice at ease.

"This is Major Braithwaite. She's here to put you to sleep for a little while." Cameron glanced at the X-rays clipped to a light board on the wall and exchanged a few words with one of the medical team.

"I'd like you to count backward from ten for me, Alice." Major Braithwaite injected something in the IV on Alice's hand, her eyes moving to a monitor.

"Ten...nine." Alice met Cameron's gaze as he pulled up his mask and tied the tapes behind his head.

"Eight." All she could see of his face were his chocolate brown eyes between his cap and his mask. What long eyelashes he had, thick and dark.

"Seven." Although she couldn't see his mouth, she knew he was smiling at her; the corners of his eyes crinkled. "Six."

He leaned closer, his hand on her shoulder. "See you on the other side," he said softly behind his mask. Then everything went dark.

Cameron pulled off his cap and mask and tossed his gloves in the trash. He held aside the plastic strip door as Alice was wheeled out of the temporary OR, still unconscious. Her arm was so slender it had seemed almost fragile as he'd set the bones. In fact there wasn't much of her at all—probably a result of spending weeks in the desert without a decent diet.

Much as he admired the work the charity did, he had mixed feelings about young women like Alice working unprotected in conflict zones—especially in countries with a misogynistic culture like this one. He didn't want her to go back out there. Lips pressed together in thought, he headed off to check on the baby.

Lt. Kelly Grace stood beside a plastic hospital bassinet, rattling a small blue rabbit in the air. "Who's a good boy?" She grinned down at the baby as Cameron moved to the other side of the crib.

"I don't need to ask if you enjoyed tending your patient."

"You know me, Cam...oops, I mean, sir."

He did know her. Very well. They'd dated for over a year way back when Cameron first came out of the Royal Military Academy Sandhurst and was stationed in Germany, back when he'd gone through something stressful and upsetting in his personal life. Kelly had been a rock, helping him through it. But they had both realized they weren't right for each other and moved on.

Cameron had started to wonder if a woman existed who was right for him. He never seemed to maintain a relationship for longer than a few months. Everything was great to start with, then his girlfriends got fed up with him being away so much and dumped him. Not that he was bothered. By that time, he had usually lost interest in them anyway.

"So how is the little guy?" The baby wore only a tiny diaper with colored alphabet bricks along the waistband. His frail body was a rich chocolate brown against the white mattress.

"He's clean and fed." Kelly patted the baby's round belly. "Look at that lovely full tummy."

Cameron touched the baby's tiny hand and smiled as he remembered the first time his own son had gripped his finger. Now George was about to turn six. Cameron was due to go home for the birthday party in a few weeks.

Where had those six years gone? Cameron would turn thirty soon, yet he had nothing except his career. Not that he didn't value his career as an army doctor— it suited him well. But there should be more to life.

He ignored the voice inside that whispered there had been more, but he'd given it away.

Kelly ran her finger over the baby's mouth with a frown. "We need to have the cleft lip repaired before we release him. Once he's turned over to an orphanage, he won't get the surgery."

"Yes, I want to take a look at that again. Will you hold him up for me?" Cameron took a penlight from his pocket as Kelly lifted the baby. She palmed the infant's head so Cameron could examine him. Gently opening the child's mouth, he shone his light inside and confirmed what he had initially suspected.

"The palate is intact." He grabbed the baby's notes and recorded his initial observations in the space that had been left for them, then added his latest findings.

Kelly deposited the child back in his bassinet while Cameron tapped his penlight on his palm. "None of our surgeons will want to take on delicate facial surgery on a baby. We need a plastic surgeon. I'm going to call my brother for advice."

"Do you want me to take the baby back to the charity worker who brought him in?"

Cameron could tell from the tone of Kelly's voice that she didn't want to give up the tiny boy just yet.

"Alice will still be groggy after her surgery. You keep the baby here for a while longer. I'll take him back when I've spoken with Radley."

Cameron pulled out his mobile phone and headed outside to stand in the shade of the doorway. He glanced at the time on the phone display. They were only an hour ahead of the UK. Radley would still be at the military hospital where he worked. Staring out at the dust blowing around the heaps of debris, he dialed his brother's number and waited.

"Lieutenant Colonel Knight," his brother answered.

"Rad, it's me."

"Please don't tell me you're not coming back for

George's birthday."

"Of course I'm coming. Why do you always assume I'm going to let you down?"

Radley grunted. "It's been known to happen."

Cameron chose to ignore that comment. He had missed George's first birthday. He hadn't been able to face playing uncle to his own son back then. Giving George up to Radley had been too fresh and painful. He was used to it now, yet it still got to him occasionally.

"We have a newborn baby here with a cleft lip."

"Not really my area of expertise."

"I know that." Why did talking to Radley always make him feel like an idiot? "I wondered if your plastic surgeon friend would help."

"Lieutenant Colonel Fabian is unlikely to fly all the way to Africa for a cleft lip, but if you can bring the child here, I'm sure he'll operate."

"Okay. Thanks, Rad. Can you mention it to him?"

"Sure. See you in a few weeks."

Cameron cut the connection and kicked at a crack in the cement. The baby would need a visa to get into the UK, and goodness knows what hoops they'd have to jump through to take the baby out of this country. He wanted to help the boy, but the whole thing was getting very complicated.

Cameron wheeled the bassinet into Alice's room to find her propped up against her pillows, sipping from a plastic cup of water.

"How's your arm?"

"Good. I'm sleepy, though."

"That'll be the sedative effect of the painkillers. It's best if you sleep for the rest of the day, anyway. I think you need to after what you've been through today."

Alice sat tall and peered towards the bassinet. "How's Sami?"

"Bathed, fed, and fast asleep." The tiny boy lay flat

out on his mattress, his small arms thrown up beside his head, a sheet over his body.

Alice relaxed into her pillows with a sigh. "What a relief. I couldn't bear it if he'd been injured."

Cameron parked the bassinet, unhooked the baby's notes from the end, and pulled a plastic chair up beside the bed. When he was seated he tapped his pen on the clipboard. "I need to take some history for him. How did he come to be in your care?"

"A group of us from Safe Cradle were working with the nomadic clans in the desert, trying to educate the women so they are more able to look after themselves and their children. The group I was with moved every day to avoid the rebels or they force the young men to join them. Early this morning the rebels caught up with us."

Alice dragged in a breath and closed her eyes, tears squeezing out and running down her cheeks. "It was awful, Cameron. Those pigs slaughtered them all— men, women, and children. I'll never forget what I saw."

Cameron gripped Alice's hand where it lay on the bedcover and gave her a moment. "How did you escape?"

"I wasn't in the main camp. They set up a birthing tent some distance away. I was there with a woman called Faiza while she gave birth." She reached out and brushed her fingers along the edge of the bassinet. "This is her son."

"So how did Faiza die?" Cameron wished he didn't need to ask. He didn't like upsetting Alice.

"Giving birth. The three women with me were meant to help her but the moment they saw the baby they wouldn't touch Faiza again or the baby. They said he was cursed because of his lip."

Cameron finally remembered he should be taking this down and hastily made some notes. He'd come across all kinds of customs and prejudices in his time working overseas with the army. Even when a people's beliefs ran contrary to his mission to preserve life, he often understood the rationale behind them, as he could here. A nomadic people living on the edge of survival would not have the resources to look after a child who needed special care.

"Do you know if the baby has any living relatives?"

"They wouldn't want him."

"I guess not. But we have to make a note if he has."

Alice shook her head sadly. "From what I saw, most everyone in the village is dead."

Cameron sucked in a breath and released it slowly. He might be in the army, but he would never get used to the persecution of civilians. It seemed to be part and parcel of just about every military conflict.

"Here's my suggestion on how we move forward. The baby obviously needs surgery to repair his lip, and he's not going to get it here. There is a plastic surgeon at the military hospital in Oxfordshire where my brother works, and he could do the operation. All we have to do is get the baby over there."

Alice visibly perked up, determination filling her blue eyes. "I'll take him. No problem."

"Unfortunately we can't just put him on an aircraft and ship him off to the UK. He needs a visa and we need to get whatever permission is necessary to take him out of this country. It would look bad if the local authorities think we are taking children without authority."

Alice sagged again, her good hand moving to rub her shoulder above her cast.

"Aching?"

"A little."

Cameron had an overwhelming urge to fold her in his arms and hug her. She was incredibly brave and had experienced things no young woman should have to cope with. But she was a patient. Much as he wanted to offer comfort, he had to maintain a professional distance. He patted her arm then pushed back his chair and moved away from the bed.

"Get some sleep. I'll make a few calls and try to arrange a visa for Sami."

It was lucky his father was a bigwig in the Ministry of Defense and quite happy to throw his weight around when necessary.

# Chapter Three

A few days later, Alice woke with a start to a booming explosion outside. The window above her head rattled, the ground shaking. Dust and flakes of cement fell from the ceiling. In the corridor, voices shouted while booted feet thudded.

Pulse racing, Alice struggled to sit up in the dark room lit only by the faint light leaking through the crack in the door. Sami started to cry, his plaintive wail rising as another boom and crash rattled the building.

"It's all right, Sami. All right, baby boy. I'm here." Alice slid out of bed and felt for her boots on the cold, rough floor.

Leaning over the bassinet, she stroked the baby's hair, speaking softly to him so he knew he wasn't alone. She wanted to cuddle him, but it was difficult to pick him up with the wretched cast covering her left arm from shoulder to wrist.

So far Lieutenant Grace had changed and fed Sami. She'd promised to help Alice work out how she could hold the baby in her lap to give him his bottle.

Another bang sounded. Flashes lit up the sky outside the small window, momentarily giving Alice a clear view of the room before leaving her blind.

Sami continued to cry, his desperate wail growing louder as the barrage of gunfire outside grew more insistent. She had to find someone to pick the baby up and soothe him. The poor little guy sounded frantic with fear.

The door burst open and light flooded the room. Cameron raced in, pulling on a utility vest. "Good, you're up. You need to get dressed quickly. We'll have a driver take you across Rejerrah to the hotel where the foreign journalists and charity workers have been evacuated." He stooped to tie his trailing boot laces. "You'll be safer there and we'll need this room for casualties."

"What's going on?"

"The rebels are shelling the airfield."

Another boom outside, closer this time, caused the whole building to shudder. The lights flickered off. After a few moments of darkness they came back on again, but not as brightly.

"The backup generator has kicked in."

"Can someone come with me to carry Sami?"

Cameron ran a hand back through his tousled hair and frowned. "We can't spare any medics. We're going to need them all. You'd best leave him here. Lieutenant Grace will have to find time to look after him."

"No. He comes with me or I stay here." After everything Alice had gone through to keep the baby safe, she was not leaving him now, especially when the hospital would be so busy it was unlikely Lieutenant Grace would have time for him.

Cameron met her gaze, firm and intense, as if judging her resolve. After a few seconds he nodded. "Okay, then. I shouldn't do this but never mind. You'll have to bunk in my room for a while." He gave a weary laugh. "I certainly won't need it for a few days."

He grabbed her clothes off the chair and heaped them on the baby's feet. "Come on. Let's move you now."

Clutching the end of the bassinet, he pushed it out

21

the door. Alice jammed her feet deeper in her boots and shuffled after him, a sheet wrapped around her thin hospital gown. She had to jog to keep up with him as he slalomed down the corridor, avoiding people and equipment. He turned at the end into a quieter area. The rooms here only had curtains over the doorways and this part of the building was in worse repair, bricks falling out of the walls in places.

Cameron pushed aside a curtain and led her into a small room with a low camp bed on one side, a chair on the other, and no windows. Bags and clothes hung from nails in the wall. She recognized the jacket with the red cross logo on the sleeve. It was the same one he'd worn when he rescued her.

"Can you manage to feed and change Sami?"

Alice glanced at the distressed baby still bawling his eyes out. "Yes," she said firmly. She would have to manage. The sterilizing unit and baby formula were in a small kitchen down the corridor, and she'd watched Lieutenant Grace prepare a bottle the previous day.

"Good. I'll see you later." Cameron grabbed his jacket and put it on, then picked up his helmet. He headed for the door but paused and looked over his shoulder. "It will be pandemonium for a while. You'll be fine. Just stay out of the way."

"I will."

He stepped out and went to draw across the door curtain.

"Cameron, be careful."

Their gazes locked. For a crazy moment she thought he would come back into the room and hug her. The moment passed and he simply nodded. Then he was gone.

Alice squatted beside the bassinet and rested a hand on Sami's tiny body, gently stroking, listening to the distant shouts and clatter of soldiers as some headed out to pick up the casualties while the others prepared.

Gradually the noise died down and so did Sami's wails.

In the light from one small table lamp, she peeled back a tape on Sami's diaper to check if it was dirty. Then she hurried along the now quiet corridors to the room where Lieutenant Grace kept the sterilizer, bottles, and formula. Alice made up a couple of bottles before dashing back to Cameron's room.

Sami was still awake, but now the barrage had died down, the baby had quieted as well. Was it simply the noise he'd reacted to, or had he sensed the tension in the people around him?

She stood the bottle on the floor beside the bed and gently wriggled her good arm beneath the baby. Bending close with her palm supporting his head, she scooped him up against her chest, his bottom resting on her cast. Pain shot up her broken arm, and she hurried to sit on the low bed.

Her years working in a women's refuge in London had given her plenty of experience handling babies. She knew it was possible for women to breast-feed while lying down. She hoped it also worked with bottle-feeding.

She lay the baby in the middle of the bed and put the nipple in his mouth. The tiny boy must have a strong survival instinct because right from the word go he had taken his bottle with no trouble. He sucked down his milk as if he knew he was lucky to have it.

When he'd finished, Alice awkwardly held him against her shoulder to burp him and settled him back in his bassinet. The shelling had stopped and an eerie silence hung over the place.

Thoughts of Cameron kept creeping into her mind. She imagined him at the airfield, shells exploding around him while he tended the wounded. Her stomach gave a sick lurch at the thought he might be hurt. Cameron Knight was not like any man she had met before. For the first time in her life, she imagined the possibility of falling in love. Something she had believed would never happen.

She glanced around the neat room at his bag and his bed. She pressed her palm to the pillow. This was where he slept, where he laid his head. Alice kicked off her boots and lifted the bedcover, then slipped underneath and settled her head on the pillow, staring up at the pockmarked cement ceiling above, imagining Cameron lying here looking at the same view.

Crazy as it seemed, in only three days she had started to care for him.

"Major Knight."

Cameron turned as a voice behind him called his name. One of the medical technicians stood in the corridor, holding aside the plastic strips that made up the door to the OR. "Lieutenant Colonel Jasper told me to pass on a message, sir."

Cameron blinked, his eyes gritty with tiredness after hours of setting broken bones, stitching wounds, and stabilizing more serious injuries so the soldiers could be safely transported back to the military hospital in the UK.

"What is it, Sergeant?" Cameron said behind his mask.

"The lieutenant colonel says you should take a break, sir."

Cameron turned back to the unconscious man on the table and tied off the last of six stitches to a laceration on the man's arm.

"Can I tell him you'll take a break, sir?"

"Yes," Cameron said without turning around. "In a few minutes. I'll just finish up here."

He examined a couple of other lacerations and put two stitches in one of them. While men were under anesthetic for more serious procedures, he took the opportunity to stitch the minor wounds. It was less stressful for them.

This poor guy had a badly traumatized leg from a blast injury. Cameron had done all he could to clean it up following the protocol his brother Radley had drawn up for removing damaged tissue and stabilizing seriously injured limbs. Whether the lower leg could be saved or not was now up to Radley back in the UK. He specialized in limb salvage.

"All right, you can take him to recovery." He was wheeled away and Cameron pulled off his bloodied plastic apron and gloves and tossed them in the trash.

He acknowledged the medical technician. "Okay, tell Jasper I'm taking a break."

The man hurried off, relief clear on his face.

Cameron followed him along the corridor, stumbling on some debris that had fallen from the wall during the bombardment. This building had once been used as offices by a freight company, but long since abandoned. That was until the NATO forces moved in and adapted it as a field hospital. It was in an ideal location close to the air field and on the right side of Rejerrah. Part of it ran back into the rocky hillside, affording extra protection.

That was where the medical staff had their quarters—where Alice and little Sami were safely tucked away from the frantic race to treat the injured servicemen.

Cameron pushed through the door into what they laughingly called the mess, a small room with a couple of tables surrounded by chairs, and a table bearing a coffee machine and ration packs.

He poured himself a tepid coffee, added dried milk and sugar, and slumped down on a chair with a ration pack in his hand. He took out a cereal bar and chewed with effort. Weariness sapped his appetite, even though he hadn't eaten for hours.

Major Braithwaite came in, her face pale and

pinched with fatigue. She silently acknowledged him, grabbed an energy drink, and hurried away again.

At times like this they were all worn down with the mental and physical stress of fighting for the lives of their fellow soldiers. Nobody had energy for social chat. Times like this left Cameron drained. It normally took him a week to recover his usual optimistic outlook on life.

His mind slipped to Alice as it had done often in the last thirty-six hours, as if she were the default setting for his thoughts when he had a moment to relax.

He pictured her as he'd left her standing in his room, wearing her boots, a pale blue hospital gown, and a white sheet wrapped around her skinny body. Her blonde hair straggled around her bumped and bruised face, her nose swollen. Yet there was something about her that tugged at him.

How was she managing with Sami? He'd asked Lieutenant Grace to check on her when she had a moment. Cameron would like to go back and see Alice himself, but he didn't have time. He didn't want the distraction; he needed to concentrate on his work.

Yet his mind focused on Alice, and he couldn't drag it away. Even now, she was probably lying in his bed. He closed his eyes and pictured her there, her blonde hair spread across his pillow. Unwanted emotions flooded up from somewhere deep inside him and wouldn't go away.

He rubbed a hand over his face and blew out a breath. He couldn't have feelings for her. It was unprofessional and inappropriate. She was his injured patient. She simply was not suitable. If he let himself develop feelings for a woman who traipsed all over the world, putting herself in danger, he would be out of his mind with worry most of the time.

And wasn't he a hypocrite?

A groan rumbled in his chest, and he pinched the

bridge of his nose.

His father was in the process of getting the baby a visa. Once the work at the hospital died down, Cameron would help Alice negotiate with the authorities so she could take Sami out of the country to the UK. Then he could forget about them and focus on his job.

Alice jolted awake and lay in the semi-darkness. Every time she turned over she woke up, either because the cast got in the way or because her arm hurt. The noise of the portable air-conditioning unit droned in the corridor, but the room was still airless and hot.

She kicked aside the thin cover and wiped sweat off her face. She wore panties, along with a T-shirt Lieutenant Grace had given her. Even though the lieutenant was busy, she had made time to check up on Alice every day to make sure she was coping with Sami. Alice liked her a lot.

She rolled over, trying to find a comfortable position for her arm. Her heart gave a little bump at the sight of Cameron lying on a sleeping bag on the floor. Her gaze traveled down his long, lean body stretched out only a few feet away from her, naked except for his underwear. The lamp in the corner of the room cast his form in light and shadow, emphasizing his toned muscles.

Relaxed in sleep, his face appeared almost boyish, the lines of worry gone. But there was nothing boyish about his biceps and the ridges of muscle in his belly. He was in good shape, but then he was a soldier. In the army, even doctors must have to train to keep fit.

Over the last three days she'd exchanged only a few words with him when they'd passed in the corridor. He had asked how she was doing, but he'd been very busy and preoccupied. She didn't think he'd slept in that time. He hadn't been back to his room anyway.

She bit her lip, uncomfortable with this situation. The poor man must be exhausted. He should have the camp bed. The temporary folding bed was just a sheet of canvas on a metal frame. Not especially comfortable, but better than the floor.

"Cameron," she whispered. He didn't stir. Not surprising, she supposed. Although she felt bad about him sleeping on the floor, it was best to let him sleep rather than wake him to change beds.

Sami whimpered and made the sucking sound she knew meant he was hungry. Alice sat up and slid off the bed. Careful not to step on Cameron, she went to the bassinet.

"Hey, sweetie, are you hungry again?" The baby had already put on weight—a born survivor. She slipped on a voluminous white gown Lieutenant Grace had given her, pushed her feet in her boots, and hurried down the corridor to fetch the bottle she had mixed up earlier. After checking the temperature, she returned to the room.

Sami's little grunts and whimpers of hunger had increased, but Cameron slept on. Alice unrolled the plastic changing mat on the bed, laid Sami on it, and changed his diaper. It was still awkward, changing him with only one good hand, but she'd honed her technique and was much quicker now.

She cleaned her hands on an antiseptic wipe and balanced the tiny boy between her crossed legs to feed him. As usual, he sucked down the contents of his bottle quickly.

"You are such a good boy, Sami." She kissed the baby's hair and stroked his cheek, smiling when his head turned towards her finger, seeking the nipple for more milk. "You'll pop if I give you any more." She lifted him up to her shoulder and rubbed his back. "Let's get those burps up so they don't give you a tummy ache."

She rocked him gently, stroking his back and humming softly. This was such a strange setup, almost surreal, living in this windowless room with a baby, trying to keep out of the way and not bother anyone. She had decided a long time ago that her mission in life was to help the vulnerable women and children who so often suffered at the hands of men—to help others avoid going through what she had suffered.

Until she found herself responsible for this poor motherless baby, she'd never had a maternal feeling in her life. Now the thought of passing him on to someone else pinched her heart.

She angled the tiny boy, cradling his head in her palm so she could see his face. He had a split in his lip that went up to his nostril and his shiny pink gum showed in the break. A disfigurement that made his clan reject him. Yet to her he was the most beautiful, special baby in the world.

His eyes had closed, already asleep after his feed. He was such a good baby. No trouble at all. This little guy had stolen her heart. Reluctantly, she settled Sami back in his bassinet and climbed in bed.

She lay on her side, her good arm underneath, and her cast rested on a pillow in front of her, the most comfortable position even though the pillow made her hot. She closed her eyes, but now she had woken she couldn't go back to sleep. Her eyes opened and her gaze strayed to Cameron. Unfamiliar sensations crept through her. It wasn't just Sami who'd stolen her heart; Cameron had touched her emotions as well. Were her feelings for this man real or just a product of the strange circumstances?

Boots echoed in the corridor outside. Low, urgent voices spoke of a medical emergency with one of the patients. As if he were specially attuned to such things, Cameron's eyes opened.

His gaze met hers and held. For long moments they

stared at each other in the shadowy room, neither saying a word. Then Cameron pushed up on an elbow.

"Do you need me?" he asked, his tone pitched low to reach the medics in the corridor but not disturb Sami.

"No, you get some sleep, Knight." It was Major Braithwaite who answered. Alice recognized the anesthetist's voice.

Cameron glanced down and noticed he was uncovered. With a mumbled apology, he pulled the sheet up over his hips before he laid his head back on the pillow.

"You should have the bed," Alice whispered.

"No, I'm fine. You learn to sleep anywhere when you're in the army."

One didn't have to be in the army to get used to that. Her mind swept back to the nights when she'd slept on the floor underneath her bed or in her toy cupboard or closet, hiding from her father.

"Sorry I more or less abandoned you," he said, rubbing his eyes. "I've lost track of how many days it's been."

"Three."

"Kelly—I mean, Lieutenant Grace—said you coped well."

"I was fine. I'm glad things have quieted down now, though." Not just because it was awful for the wounded soldiers who'd been through the hospital, but because she had missed Cameron.

A question popped into Alice's head. Normally she wouldn't dream of asking him such a personal thing, but in the intimate darkness of the small room, they felt more like friends than doctor and patient. "Is Kelly your girlfriend?"

Cameron's gaze sharpened as if the question woke him up. "She used to be, but not anymore."

"Ahh." That explained why they seemed to be close.

"I was going to tell you tomorrow, my father sent

across a visa for Sami. He can legally enter the UK now."

"That's great." She didn't ask how Cameron's father had managed such a thing so quickly. She was just relieved he had. "I need to go to the government offices in Rejerrah and inquire about taking him out of the country for medical treatment."

"Do you speak the language?"

"Just enough to get by."

"I'll come with you. I'm pretty good with languages, and I don't like the idea of you going on your own."

"Thanks, Cameron."

He grinned. "You're welcome." He reached up and ran a finger along her forearm. That simple touch sent tingling fire streaking across her skin.

His grin fell away and they stared at each other, his brown eyes dark and mysterious in the low light.

"Best get some more sleep," Cameron said.

Alice nodded, a flurry of mixed emotions charging through her. She liked Cameron, really liked him. If she had met him under different circumstances, she might have wanted to explore these feelings she had for him. But right now Sami had to be her first and only priority.

# Chapter Four

"You're a maverick, Major. You don't follow the rules," Lieutenant Colonel Jasper said, frowning.

Cameron sat across the desk from his commanding officer in a tiny room with one wall half-demolished after the recent bombardment. Dust coated everything, even though they'd tried to clean up.

He'd come here to tell Jasper that he'd let Alice and Sami bunk in his room while the hospital was busy, deciding it was best to come clean rather than wait for Jasper to find out from someone else.

"It's only because you're such a good doctor that you get away with it."

Cameron knew Jasper was right, although he preferred to think of himself as a dedicated doctor. He only ever broke rules to help his patients. He might be an army officer, but he was a doctor first. Patients came before rules. Fighting to save lives on a daily basis had a way of focusing the mind on what was important in life. Usually it wasn't a rule dreamed up by a bureaucrat in the Ministry of Defense.

The lieutenant colonel flattened his palm on the desk and stared at it for a moment. "Is the girl still bunking in your room?"

"No, sir. As soon as we had the space, I moved her back onto the ward. This morning, actually."

"Good. Then we'll say no more about it." He straightened and cleared his throat. "Let's move on to other business. I hear your brother has been promoted to colonel. I'm not at all surprised. An exceptional man, your brother. I served with him in Afghanistan a few years ago. He impressed me greatly."

Cameron smiled. "I hadn't heard. That's great." And it was. But a strange hollow feeling punched through his solar plexus. All his life he'd tried to match up to his older brother. He'd thought if he worked hard and did his best, he would be as good as Radley. It never worked out that way.

Radley had something special, a star quality that set him apart—and Cameron didn't have it. He was the one who screwed up and let his parents down.

Radley traveled the world speaking at medical symposia about his limb-salvage techniques. He had the glittering career, the beautiful wife, and the lovely children. He even had Cameron's son.

Cameron averted his gaze, perturbed by his flash of resentment. He'd thought he'd come to terms with the situation years ago. Although he loved his son, he hadn't been ready to be a husband and father. He'd accepted that George would grow up thinking Radley was his father while Cameron played the part of uncle. Every time he returned to the UK on leave, he made a point of seeing his son.

Maybe it was being around Alice and Sami that had stirred up Cameron's feelings again. He didn't want to dwell on this. He should have put the issue behind him long ago.

"I'd like permission to take a couple of hours to accompany Alice Conway to the government building. She wants to take the orphaned baby with the cleft lip back to the UK for treatment. My father has secured a visa but we're not sure what the legalities are on this end."

"Best if you ride with one of the patrols. Things are a little sticky after the recent bombardment. Some of the locals blame NATO for the escalation in the attacks. They don't want to admit the rebels would have overrun the city months ago if we weren't here."

Cameron stood. "Thank you, sir. Good suggestion."

He headed for the door to take Alice the news. Although he tried to focus on the issue of Sami, thoughts of his son still drifted through the back of his mind, memories of when he was a tiny baby, of the excitement Cameron had felt the first time he saw him and realized the baby boy was his.

Cameron turned into an empty room, closed his eyes, and pressed his back against the rough stone wall. He sucked in a couple of deep breaths and blew them out, willing himself to relax and let his remorse go. He didn't want to feel like this when he went home on leave for George's birthday. His relatives were bound to pick up on his mood. Despite his feelings, he knew he'd made the right decision for his son. Radley was a much better father than Cameron could ever hope to be.

Alice stepped out of the field hospital into the blistering heat, the sky unbroken blue, stretching to the horizon. Across the desert, the ramshackle tents and cabins of the refugee camp formed a jumbled pattern against a backdrop of distant mountains.

Cameron put a hand under her elbow and pointed at a sandy-colored military vehicle parked a short distance away. One soldier was already on top, manning a gun.

"We're going in the Foxhound. I'll ride up front," Cameron said. "You go in the back. It's probably safer."

She climbed in and shuffled past the legs of the gunner, then pulled down a folding seat behind the driver and sat down. Under her voluminous floor-length robe that covered her T-shirt and shorts,

Cameron had strapped up her cast in a sling. It helped ease the ache in her shoulder.

Cameron hopped in the front passenger seat and dumped his medical backpack on the floor near her. She leaned forward to see out the windshield, scrunching the fabric of her robe in her hand nervously. She had expected to catch a taxi to the government building, not ride with a patrol. This seemed a little over the top.

Another two soldiers got in and sat down, their guns across their knees.

"Do you expect trouble?" she asked.

The driver glanced over his shoulder. "Don't you worry, love. An explosive device could go off right underneath us and we'd still survive. This vehicle is a great piece of engineering."

She smiled tentatively, far from reassured.

Cameron reached back and squeezed her hand with a nod of encouragement. The engine rumbled to life and the vehicle pulled away.

Alice hung on as the Foxhound bumped into potholes and weaved between heaps of rubbish and rubble, heading away from the air base and hospital to the main part of Rejerrah. They joined the busy road around the city. Men on motor scooters and in old beaten-up cars raced every which way. Dust rose in plumes from the tires; Alice tasted it gritty and dry on her tongue.

The squat stone and cement buildings lining the road looked half-finished or half-demolished, she wasn't sure which, many with corrugated-iron roofs.

The Foxhound turned into the old city and threaded its way through narrower roads, frequently having to slow down for people. Old men with donkeys piled high with bundles trudged along in the middle of the road, and women in brightly colored robes walked with babies wrapped on their fronts or backs.

"We're heading over there." Cameron pointed.

Through the dust drifting in the air, Alice made out taller buildings in the center of Rejerrah.

"I landed at the commercial airport on the other side of the city when I arrived." That seemed like a lifetime ago now, not just four months. She had been naive and unprepared for the living conditions in the desert with the nomads, or the brutal reality of the war. She'd witnessed terrible things that would stay with her forever.

What had happened to the others from Safe Cradle who'd come with her? Three teams flew in, destined to work with different nomadic groups. She'd discovered that the two women who had been working with her had both been airlifted to safety shortly before the rebels attacked. They hadn't come to find her. Maybe they hadn't had time.

Alice leaned forward and rested a hand on Cameron's shoulder. "You said the charity workers were evacuated to a hotel?"

"Yes. All the foreign nationals were rounded up about a week ago. The hotel's on the other side of Rejerrah, near the commercial airport. I expect a lot of them have been flown out by now."

Alice had only joined the charity a month before she came out here. She wondered briefly if they could help her arrange for Sami to leave the country. But she'd been the junior member of her team, and they hadn't exactly looked after her. She trusted Cameron far more, despite the fact he was not only a man but a soldier—something she would never have believed possible a few months ago.

A loud crash pulled her back to the moment and set her heart racing. The corporal in charge of the patrol shouted orders and a second soldier stood and manned a gun sticking out the top of the vehicle, but they didn't slow down.

"It's all right," Cameron said after a few tense moments. "Just kids throwing rocks."

The men seemed to settle down again, and Alice's pulse returned to near normal. They entered an area that was obviously a business district with taller buildings. Many of them looked abandoned.

The Foxhound slowed outside a three-story cement building with burn marks up the walls and boarded-up windows on one side. Alice spoke a little of the language but couldn't read it, so the words painted on the front meant nothing to her.

"Here you are," the corporal driving said. "We'll wait for you."

Cameron jumped out and extended a hand to help Alice down. She folded the white fabric over her head and Cameron tucked it in. They had already decided it was best to cover her blonde hair.

"So are we going to start with their version of Child Protective Services, or the emigration office?" Cameron asked. They had researched the local government structure and identified these two departments to contact.

"Child Protective Services. They deal with orphanages and adoptions."

"Okay."

Cameron led the way inside a dimly lit entrance foyer. A hot, stale smell filled the place—totally foreign and unwelcoming.

Some people lined up at a desk while others sat along the wall on wooden benches. The man behind the desk was arguing with the guy at the front of the line, both shouting and gesturing.

Back at the hospital, when they discussed this trip, Alice had been hopeful. Now they were here, her heart dropped to her boots. Suddenly negotiating this foreign system seemed like a nightmare.

The two men who'd been arguing fell silent as they

noticed Cameron in his uniform. Everyone stared. The man behind the desk rose and approached, firing questions.

Alice's minimal grasp of the language was useless. She had no idea what he was saying, and he didn't look friendly.

Lucky for them, Cameron obviously did understand the man. He answered calmly and confidently. The man's belligerence faded and he directed Cameron to some stairs.

"Well, we're in the right place." He led the way upstairs.

"What did the man say?" Alice asked.

"He was defensive at first. I think he thought I'd come to cause trouble. When I told him why we were here, he calmed down." Cameron halted on the second landing and looked around. "Here we are." He knocked on a door and opened it.

Two men sat at scarred wooden desks heaped with brown folders. More folders were stacked against the walls, many with the contents hanging out.

Cameron spoke to the officials and obviously answered some questions. Eventually one of them searched in a drawer and pulled out a form.

Alice took the offered document, glancing at the unreadable text. "What's this for?"

"The only way they'll let you take Sami out of the country is if you adopt him. That's what the form's for."

Alice's heart leaped and fluttered in her chest like a trapped bird. Adopt Sami? She had hardly let herself imagine she might be able to do this. It was what she wanted, more than anything else in the world.

Sitting down at an empty desk, she pushed aside some papers. Cameron took a pen from his pocket and held it out. "Do you want me to translate for you?"

"Yes, please." She tamped down the excitement bubbling inside her. This was only the start of the process. She had no idea how long they would make her wait before she could bring Sami to the UK. They might even turn her down. This was not the time to think that. Be positive, she told herself.

Cameron leaned over her. "Name and address," he said, running his finger over the words.

Alice wrote and Cameron translated: her age, twenty-six; her educational qualifications, college diploma in social work; her home address, London, England. They seemed to want to know everything except her shoe size. Thirty minutes later when she had finished, she signed the form with a flourish and handed it back to Cameron, her heart racing.

"Will you tell them he needs surgery? I want to take him home as quickly as possible."

"I have already. I don't think they usually allow people to walk in off the street and fill out adoption forms. Officers who work in the orphanages normally have to recommend you. The fact Sami needs surgery is why they've bent the rules."

Cameron placed the form on the man's desk, but he shook his head and tapped his finger on Alice's signature. Cameron exchanged a few sentences with the government official, then his lips thinned.

"What's the matter?" Alice was light-headed with tension, her emotions swinging from excitement to fear that they would turn her down.

"He says you can't sign the form."

"I don't understand. Who does sign it then?"

"Your husband."

Alice stared at Cameron, totally confused, sure she had missed something. "I don't have a husband."

"He wanted me to sign the form," Cameron said. "He thought I was your husband. They only allow married couples to adopt children here. It's one of the rules."

Alice pressed a hand over her mouth, her gaze fixed

on Cameron's suddenly guarded expression.

"I can't leave Sami here in an orphanage. I won't."

"I agree. I haven't visited an orphanage but I can guess what the conditions are like."

"Will you sign then, please? Pretend to be my husband?"

Cameron dropped his gaze on a sigh. "I wish I could. The trouble is I've already told him you aren't married. The only way he'll believe us now is if we can show him a marriage certificate."

Cameron stood on top of the hill behind the field hospital and stared across Rejerrah. The ubiquitous dust hung over the city like a pall of smoke, but he could still make out the tall buildings in the business district where he and Alice had visited the government office the previous day.

He swiveled to gaze over the desert, to the shamble of tents and huts that marked the refugee camp. About five miles farther out was the wrecked rebel jeep that had been chasing Alice down, and the place on the rocky ground where she'd fallen holding Sami, just before he got to them.

And here he was in the middle with a huge conundrum. He wanted to do his best for Sami. Even if someone else had brought the baby to the hospital, he would still have gone out of his way to help the tiny boy. But because it was Alice, he wanted to help even more. Yet to marry her just to get the child out of the country felt like going way above and beyond the call of duty.

He sat on a rock and rubbed a hand over his sweaty face. The sun beat down relentlessly, burning the tops of his ears. He should cover them up. He should go back inside. Yet he didn't move. Alice was inside fretting over Sami's fate. Cameron couldn't bear to see her worrying when he had the power to do something about it.

Perhaps God was giving him this chance to help Sami so he could make up for not being a father to George? Or perhaps he was trying to find hidden depths in a straightforward situation. When it came down to basics, it was a simple decision—he could either marry Alice and take Sami back to the UK for surgery, or let the baby sink without trace in a lousy orphanage.

The sound of a helicopter drew his attention and he shaded his eyes to watch as it approached the airfield on his left. The Apache raised a hurricane of dust, obscuring itself as it neared the ground. Cameron pressed his sleeve over his nose and narrowed his eyes as the edge of the dust cloud hit him.

"Cam, there you are."

Cameron turned to find Kelly Grace trudging up the hill behind him. She reached the top and rested a hand on his shoulder. "Move over so I can sit down."

Cameron shuffled along with a sigh; so much for getting away from everyone to think in peace.

She rubbed his arm. "I'm worried about you."

Kelly knew him better than most people and he trusted her. She was the only person he had confided in about this problem. Perhaps talking the situation over with her was a good idea.

"You don't have to marry Alice," she said. "Nobody will stop her taking the baby out on a military flight now she has a UK entry visa for the boy."

"Yeah, I know. But how's it going to look to the authorities at home if she takes the baby out of this country without proper authorization? That will nix any chance she has of adopting him. Sure, Sami will get his surgery and be allowed to stay in the UK, but not with Alice. Even with my father's influence, I doubt Social Services would let her keep him."

"I can understand why she wants to keep him."

Kelly's gaze drifted into the distance. "I'd feel the same way."

Cameron wiped his sweaty palms on his knees. Alice hadn't asked him to marry her, but they both knew it was the only way to take Sami out of the country legally. Well, almost legally. He supposed a marriage on paper just to con the system wasn't strictly legal.

Kelly fell uncharacteristically quiet for a while.

"So, what do you think?" Cameron prompted. "If you've got any other suggestions, I'm all ears."

"Do you have feelings for her?" She cast him a quick sideways glance.

Suddenly this conversation felt awkward. They had stopped dating years ago, but there was an edge to Kelly's voice that made him uncomfortable.

"I admire her, and I don't want to see her hurt." He rubbed a hand across his mouth, trying to think how to explain what he felt. That was difficult when he didn't know himself. But he was certain about some things. "I want to make sure Sami gets his operation, and that Alice has the chance to adopt him in the UK."

"There's your answer, then. You marry her."

Emotion shot through Cameron, hot and uncomfortable, although quite what emotion it was he couldn't say. If marrying Alice was the only way to help her keep Sami, he would have to do it. "I'd better call the padre and arrange things quickly. It makes sense for us to travel to the UK together next week when I go home for George's birthday."

"Your parents are going to be surprised."

"That's got to be the understatement of the century."

# Chapter Five

Alice stood in front of the army padre in her shorts, borrowed T-shirt, and boots, with ugly yellow and purple bruising around her eyes and a nose that was still somewhat swollen.

The room was small, with flaking cement walls and holes for windows. A makeshift place of worship in this hostile environment. The only thing identifying its purpose was a metal cross on a wooden stand set on a table behind Father Dudley.

Cameron stood at Alice's side wearing his desert camouflage trousers, dusty boots, and a sandy-colored T-shirt. Lieutenant Grace and Major Braithwaite sat on wooden chairs behind them, both there to witness the marriage.

*Marriage!*

Alice swallowed down the massive lump in her throat as memories from the past rushed back. She had sworn never to marry. She had believed she would never trust a man enough to commit like that. If someone had told her she would marry a soldier in a makeshift chapel in a war zone, she would have thought they were crazy.

Yet here she was, and far from being nervous with Cameron she was deeply grateful to him. She cast a quick sideways glance at the gorgeous army doctor with his warm brown eyes and easy smile. She might be developing feelings for him, but Alice had no illusions he was interested in her. When he'd suggested they marry, he had made it clear it was only so they could help Sami.

His lack of interest didn't surprise her. She looked a mess. She was definitely not much of a catch. What did surprise her was that a man like Cameron didn't have a wife or girlfriend at home already.

The pleasant tenor of the padre's voice repeated the familiar words of the marriage ceremony. Alice responded appropriately where needed, her voice faint with nerves, her senses reeling at the strangeness of the situation.

"I now pronounce you man and wife. You may kiss the bride," Father Dudley said.

Alice's gaze shot to Cameron in alarm. Considering the circumstances, she had assumed they would skip this part of the ceremony.

He turned to face her. As if in a dream, her feet stepped around too. She met his gaze, and he smiled intimately, as if the two of them shared a secret. The smile confused her, set her mind racing to understand what he was thinking.

"Alice," he said softly, raising a hand to rest on her good shoulder. Then he leaned down, hesitated a moment, and pressed his lips to hers.

The kiss lasted only a few seconds, a chaste touch of his lips to hers. Yet the warm grip of his fingers on her shoulder and the firm touch of his lips on hers rocked her foundations as surely as if a shell had dropped on the chapel.

She had been certain he was only being kind, trying to help her adopt Sami, certain he wasn't attracted to her. After the kiss, she wondered if she were wrong. Then he turned back to the padre, all business again.

They each signed the marriage certificate and had it

witnessed, then Cameron folded the piece of paper carefully and put it in his pocket. He ushered her outside into the jeep that had brought them across the airfield to the main area of the NATO base.

Alice sat in the back with Lieutenant Grace and Major Braithwaite while Cameron took the front seat beside the driver. The others chatted and joked but Alice stayed silent, her thoughts spinning with confusion over how she felt and what would happen next.

She was married to Maj. Cameron Knight.

For the first time it occurred to her that she knew next to nothing about this man apart from his profession. He was obviously bright and well educated, otherwise he wouldn't be a doctor. He'd mentioned his father worked at the Ministry of Defense, and he had a brother who was also an army doctor.

What would his military family think of her? Would she even meet them? After all, she and Cameron were married in name only.

Alice felt light-headed with unreality as the jeep pulled up outside the field hospital. Cameron jumped out and his colleagues followed. Alice slid along the seat to reach the open door, awkward because of her broken arm. Suddenly Cameron was there, his hand outstretched to support her and help her climb out.

"Thank you," she said, self-conscious in a way she hadn't been before the wedding.

"You're welcome." He dropped his steadying grip the moment she found her feet and joined his colleagues again, resuming their conversation.

Alice followed them inside, her emotions swinging around like a weather vane in a storm. The marriage was not real. There was no relationship between them. So why did she now feel shy and uncertain around Cameron like a schoolgirl with a crush?

She needed to stop thinking about him and focus on

Sami. She strode past Cameron and his two friends and hurried back to her room where she had left Sami asleep in his bassinet. The nurse on duty was just leaving the room when she entered.

"How's he been?"

"As good as gold. You'll probably want to prepare a bottle. I think he's waking up."

Alice leaned over the bassinet and smiled down at her baby boy. She couldn't pinpoint exactly when she'd started to think of Sami as *her* baby, but he absolutely was hers. She would do whatever it took to make sure her little boy was safe, healthy, and loved. That meant taking him back to the UK with her, arranging for the surgery on his lip, and officially adopting him in Britain.

Cameron caught her up and came into the room. "You were anxious to get back here."

"I'm always anxious to see this little guy." Alice stroked Sami's cheek. He waved his arms and kicked his legs.

"He recognizes you," Cameron said.

Sami turned his head in Cameron's direction and made his cute huffing sound.

"He recognizes you as well, or at least your voice."

Cameron pressed his lips together thoughtfully and stepped up beside the bassinet. He stared down at Sami then touched his fingertips to the baby's cheek, a smile pulling at his lips. Sami's little legs kicked like crazy. "I think you're right," Cameron said. "He does know me."

He ran his fingers over the baby's chest and arms. "You're growing so fast, you funny little guy." His gaze lingered on the baby for a few moments longer then he turned his attention to Alice. "Are you going to feed him now?"

At her nod, he lifted the baby out of his bassinet and cradled him in an arm. "Let's go and prepare your bottle then, bud."

Alice headed for the small kitchen where the bottle warmer and formula were kept, Cameron and Sami at her side. Her heart raced every time she glanced at the baby, so tiny in Cameron's tanned, muscular arms. He'd picked up the baby before, but always as a doctor to examine him. This time was different. Was Cameron growing attached to Sami?

Alice quickly mixed up the bottle and they went back to the room. She sat on the bed and took Sami from Cameron then put the nipple in the hungry baby's mouth. Cameron crossed his arms and observed, an amused smile on his lips, as Sami sucked down his milk.

"Well, I can't stand here watching him all day. I'm going to join a patrol and return to the government offices with this." He patted the pocket where he had stowed the marriage certificate. "Wish me luck with the Child Protective Services people."

"Of course." She would do more than wish him luck. She would be praying for success the whole time he was away.

Cameron flicked up his eyebrows and grinned. "See you later." He turned and strode out the door.

After Cameron left, it took a good few minutes for Alice's heart rate to return to normal. When Sami was burped, she laid him on the bed and stretched out at his side, kissing his sweet little face. "I'm going to be your mummy soon," she whispered. Then with a furtive glance at the door to make sure nobody was listening, she continued. "And Cameron is going to be your daddy."

Cameron strode along the walkway down the center of the RAF C-17 Aeromed aircraft that he, Alice, Sami, and a group of soldiers heading home for rest and relaxation had boarded to head back to the UK.

The plane had brought in supplies and then been

adapted to carry out wounded. This time there were only four casualties to take home, all men Cameron had worked on in the field hospital.

This was an RAF operation, with a full staff of doctors and medical technicians manning the plane. Cameron was officially off duty, but he couldn't twiddle his thumbs for over five hours when he might be of help.

"Captain Fellows, can I assist?" Cameron addressed the nearest doctor, then put his hands on his hips and scanned the area where the patients were, two of them on life support machines.

"Thanks for the offer, but I think we're on top of things." The young captain nodded past Cameron towards the seats occupied by the other passengers. "Perhaps you should get back to your bride."

Cameron had hoped to keep the wedding quiet but the news had spread around the base like wildfire. His commanding officer had appeared to be at a loss for words, which suited Cameron fine. He glanced over his shoulder to where Alice had her attention firmly fixed on Sami in his traveling crib on the ground in front of her. Her braided hair hung forward, gleaming in the lights like gold.

"If I were you, I'd have other things on my mind besides work," the young captain said.

That was the problem. Cameron did have other things on his mind. Inappropriate things considering the marriage was in name only. Ever since the wedding ceremony two days ago, he'd started to notice Alice in a way he hadn't before. Maybe he had a mental block that labeled female patients as off limits, and that had been lifted. He gave the man a weak smile. "Okay. Well, you know where I am if you need me."

He turned and wandered to a storage unit and grabbed an armful of ration packs. The last thing he felt like was food, but it might distract him. "Anyone for

48

some lunch?"

Most of the soldiers answered in the affirmative and he tossed the ration packs to them, before grabbing a couple for Alice and himself.

"They don't need you then?" she asked as he sat at her side. The bruising around her eyes had finally faded. Her blue eyes looked bigger and her previously swollen nose was now small and very cute.

To make matters worse, he had realized there was no way he could simply file for an annulment of the marriage on the grounds of non-consummation. He was the one who'd signed the adoption papers. If they dissolved the marriage, it would mess up any likelihood that the British courts would ratify the existing adoption. Alice would then have to start again from scratch.

Until the adoption was finalized in the UK, the marriage must appear to be real. He had no idea how she would feel about that. They needed to talk the issue over soon.

"Are you sure you're happy to come to my brother's?" In this situation, it seemed sensible that he and Alice should stay together with Sami. His relatives would be only too happy to meet Alice and the baby. They might not be quite so overjoyed when they discovered the circumstances of the marriage.

"That would be great, if they don't mind."

"Did you want to go and see your parents over the weekend?"

Alice ducked her head and sorted through her ration pack.

"Is there a problem, Alice?" He'd noticed she avoided talking about her parents.

She flashed him an oblique look that he couldn't decipher. "Dad's busy. I don't want to trouble him. I'll call my mum sometime."

Alice had been out of the country in a war zone for

months, yet she thought her father wouldn't have time for her?

Normally he wouldn't pry into someone's personal life, but this was different. Alice was his wife. "You don't get along with your father?"

She shrank down in her seat and hugged her ration pack. "I don't want him to know about Sami."

"Okay." Warning bells sounded in Cameron's head. Her expression closed off at the mention of her father. He wanted to know why. It occurred to him that he had no idea what sort of a background Alice came from. He knew nothing about her except her nationality and that she hailed from the London area like him.

"I'll need to notify Social Services about Sami when we arrive back," she said, obviously aiming to deflect any further questions about her father.

"My sister-in-law is a lawyer. She specializes in family law. I expect she can help us."

Cameron had a nasty suspicion the Social Services people weren't going to like the fact they had brought a foreign orphan into the country without being vetted as adoptive parents first. He hoped it didn't count against them too much.

It was a good thing he had a close, well-connected family. Cameron was no social worker, but he guessed Social Services were a lot more likely to let Alice keep the baby if she stayed in a supportive family environment.

Alice leaned down and rested her hand on Sami's chest as if drawing strength from her connection with the boy. "Are you sure your family won't mind putting me and Sami up?"

Cameron wanted to keep them with him, and it wasn't just because of the adoption. He wanted to make sure Sami was all right, and monitor Alice's arm. That's what he told himself, anyway.

"Heck, no." Cameron laughed. "My mother will be

over the moon to meet him. You should have seen her with her first grandchild. She wouldn't put George down."

"Is George your brother's son?"

"Yes." Cameron clamped his lips together. Why had he mentioned George? He didn't want to discuss him. He'd only end up revealing how he'd given up his own son to his brother. He didn't need to be a mind reader to know Alice wouldn't approve.

# Chapter Six

With nothing but the clothes on her back and her passport, Alice felt almost naked in the arrivals hall at Brize Norton military airport. At the field hospital, it hadn't mattered that she had nothing. Everything was so primitive there. Back here in England, in the heart of civilization, everything was different.

She brushed at the dust on her clothes, self-conscious when she noticed the women in colorful summer dresses there to welcome home their husbands.

"Everyone else has a bag. I feel weird with nothing."

"Don't worry," Cameron said. "We'll make sure you have everything you need when we get to my brother's place."

She hadn't taken much with her to Africa. Her important belongings like her bank cards were stashed at the women's refuge in London where she had volunteered while she was at college. As soon as she could, she planned to visit her old friend Maeve who ran the refuge, collect her stuff, and introduce Cameron, if he were interested in coming.

More of her things remained in her old bedroom at her parents' house, but she had no intention of going there, even though she would like her mother to see Sami. It wasn't worth the risk. Her mother could never keep a secret from her father. If he found out Alice was trying to adopt a baby, he would interfere.

A tearful woman ran forward and hugged a soldier they had traveled with. He picked up his little girl and swung her around, making her giggle. What must it be like to have a real marriage with a man who loved you and his children? Alice couldn't even imagine.

"I'll call my brother and see where he is." Cameron had his bag in one hand and Sami's carrier in the other. He put them down on the floor next to a seat so Alice could sit beside Sami. Then he pressed his mobile phone to his ear, wandering back and forth, absently rubbing his chin.

"Rad, we've landed," he said.

A long sigh of relief whispered between Alice's lips. She gently rubbed her sleeping baby, who was oblivious to the fact he was now on British soil. She had been so fearful for Sami's safety. If the authorities in his homeland had taken him from her, he likely wouldn't have survived.

"My brother will be here in five. He's just entered the gates." Cameron sat beside her and leaned over to peer at Sami. "Is the little guy okay?"

"Still asleep." She held aside the edge of the bag to give Cameron a view of Sami.

"How about you?" Cameron raised a hand and stroked some loose strands of hair back from her face.

Her pulse leaped. Every time he touched her she couldn't think straight. A strange woolly sensation filled her head, and she went all tingly. Part of her longed for his touch, yet another part of her wished he would keep his distance and stop confusing her. This wasn't real. Their supposed relationship was all pretense. Yet she had difficulty remembering that when he appeared to be so caring.

"Ah, there's Radley." Cameron jumped up and strode towards a man in army uniform. They embraced, both laughing and thumping each other on the back.

"Glad to see you home in one piece," Radley said, throwing an arm around Cameron's shoulders. The likeness between the two men was amazing. Radley was an inch or two taller than Cameron, with the same dark hair, brown eyes, and easy smile.

Alice rose as they approached, a tentative smile on her lips.

"You must be Alice." Radley extended a hand and shook hers firmly. "Nice to meet you." His gaze flicked to her arm before returning to her face. "I gather you had a close shave with the rebel forces. I bet you're pleased to be home."

Alice nodded. "Thank you for picking us up."

"No problem." Radley smacked the back of Cameron's head playfully. "Had to pick up the little brother anyway."

Sami chose that moment to wake and let out a thin wail of hunger. Radley bent over the bag, his expression softening. "This must be the baby you want Fabian to see." He moved the cover away from Sami's mouth so he could see his lip. "Any fissure in the soft palate?"

"No, just the lip," Cameron answered.

"In that case, Fabian should be able to operate immediately. Probably the sooner the better."

Alice's heart skipped a beat. She gripped Sami's tiny hand, relief mingled with nerves that her baby was to have an operation.

Radley must have noticed her expression because he smiled reassuringly. "Nothing to worry about. Lieutenant Colonel Fabian is one of the best plastic surgeons in the world."

Cameron moved to her side, put an arm around her, and angled his head close. "It's a routine procedure. All Sami will have is a tiny scar."

Alice leaned the side of her head on his shoulder,

instinctively accepting the comfort he offered. She might have only known him for a few weeks, but it seemed like longer. Being thrown together in such extreme circumstances had brought them close.

He had been wonderful, supportive, and helpful. It would be great to stay with him, to have someone on her side, someone who would put himself out to help her.

Radley's amused chuckle drew her gaze. "Olivia was fretting over the sleeping arrangements, worrying if we had enough bedrooms what with Mum and Dad coming for the weekend as well. Looks like you two will be happy to share a room."

Alice tensed, heat streaking through her body and bursting in her cheeks. Cameron would have to tell his brother that they weren't really a couple, yet she had been enjoying the pretense.

Cameron's arm tightened around her shoulders. "That's fine," he said. "Of course we'll share. I guess you'll find out soon enough, so I might as well tell you now—Alice is my wife."

Alice sat in the back of Radley's large black 4x4 beside Sami, who was strapped in a luxury baby seat that belonged to Radley's baby daughter.

Her thoughts churned, her emotions swinging all over the place. Cameron had told his brother they were married, but he hadn't explained their temporary arrangement. Now Cameron's family would believe the marriage was the real thing.

Why had he lied? Did he worry his parents wouldn't accept her and Sami if they knew the truth? Was it possible he really had feelings for her?

No, that was just wishful thinking.

Alice rubbed her temples. Too many wild thoughts swirled in her head. She didn't know if she was pleased or upset. Now they would have to maintain the pretense in front of people who knew Cameron, and could tell when he lied. All she'd wanted was help to bring her baby boy here. Everything seemed to be getting out of hand.

Her eyelids fell and she yawned, suddenly overwhelmed with fatigue after the long day of traveling. In the front, Cameron and Radley discussed the progress of the conflict in Africa. The pleasant timbre of their deep masculine voices washed over her and she dozed.

"Nearly there," Cameron said after a while.

She opened her eyes to see him looking back at her between the seats. "You can have a nap when we get to Radley's, if you like. I'll look after Sami."

"I'll see how I feel." Alice smiled and Cameron reached back and squeezed her knee. He had helped her with Sami, but it was the first time he had offered to look after him. She was pleased but uncertain as well. They needed to discuss this fake marriage and lay the ground rules so she knew what to expect.

The car glided along a narrow country road with bushy hedges on either side and colorful wildflowers scattered among the green grass. Radley turned the car between two stone pillars and the tires crunched up a gravel drive between borders of shrubs and flowers before swinging around to park in front of a large country house.

"Home," Radley said, a smile in his voice. He jumped out and strode towards the front door. A tall, elegant woman with long dark hair stepped out carrying a baby girl. He enclosed them in his arms and kissed the woman and baby, then they exchanged a few words and both looked at the car.

Alice dropped her gaze, embarrassed to be caught watching them so closely. Radley seemed to be much like Cameron—a kind man, one who cared about his family.

The car door opened, and Cameron unclipped Sami from the baby seat and lifted him out. Alice climbed out too and stretched as Cameron stopped beside her. "I expect you'd like to carry the little guy in." He passed the sleepy baby across, careful to make sure she had a secure hold on him with her good arm before letting go. "I'll get the bags."

Before he could move to the trunk, a little boy dashed out of the front door. "Uncle Cam, Uncle Cam."

Cameron whooped, picked up the child, and swung him around, a grin on his face. "How's my favorite boy?"

"All right. Have you brought me a present?"

"That's not very polite, George." Radley's wife frowned and strode over to them with an embarrassed shake of her head. "Presents tomorrow, young man." She leaned in and kissed Cameron's cheek while he hugged her son.

"Hi, Livi. This rascal keeping you on your toes?"

She rolled her eyes but it was plain she adored her little boy.

Cameron kissed the soft dark curls on top of the baby girl's hair and tweaked her pink hair clip. "How's my pretty little niece?"

"Emma's fine, aren't you, sweetie." Olivia hefted the girl higher to see Cameron, but she buried her face in her mother's neck. "Just a little shy, as you can see."

Cameron stepped over to Alice, George hanging on his hand. "Olivia, this is Alice, my wife."

Olivia's eyes opened like saucers, and she choked on her greeting. She pressed a hand over her mouth, her startled gaze fixed on Alice. "I had no idea you were married."

After a few awkward seconds she seemed to recover. A genuine smile of pleasure replaced the shock. She leaned in and kissed Alice's cheek. "Wow. It's lovely to meet the woman who has finally made Cameron commit. I didn't think it would ever happen."

Olivia beamed at her as though she had won the lottery. A flush swept over Alice. She hated deceiving Cameron's relatives.

Alice pushed aside her guilt and composed herself. "It's nice to meet you. Thank you for putting me up. I really appreciate it."

Tall and elegant in tailored cream pants and a floral blouse, her long hair thick and shiny, Olivia was slightly intimidating. She looked like a model. In comparison, Alice resembled something the cat had dragged in and left on the mat.

Olivia angled her head to see Sami's face. "This little man is obviously the baby you rescued. He's very young to have flown so far. How'd he handle the trip?"

"No problem at all. Although I think he's ready for a bottle. He woke up at the airport, but the car ride sent him to sleep again."

Olivia glanced over her shoulder to where Radley had joined in the roughhousing with Cameron and George. "Remember, George is only five," she said to the men.

"I'm six tomorrow, Mummy," the boy shouted.

"Nearly grown up then." Cameron tossed the squealing boy in the air and caught him.

"Come on," Olivia said, grabbing the baby bag from the trunk. "Let's leave the boys to play."

The two women walked side by side towards the house, both cuddling their babies. Alice followed Olivia through the front door. A vase of lilies sat on a hall table and their fragrance filled the room.

A wide staircase rose in the center of the hall. Olivia started up it. "Radley mentioned that you want to adopt Sami in the UK. I'm a lawyer and have worked on similar cases. It's actually against the law to bring a foreign child into the UK for adoption if you haven't been approved by an adoption agency, but I think

Cameron's father has already smoothed that out." She glanced back with a conspiratorial smile. "It's useful having a father-in-law who works for the MOD. He has the ear of some very important people. All we need to do is get you an appointment with an adoption agency so you and Cameron can be approved to adopt. Until then, you should be able to foster Sami."

Olivia made the adoption process sound easy. Alice hoped it would be. If anyone tried to take Sami away from her she wasn't sure what she'd do, but she wouldn't give her baby up.

"Here you are." Olivia pushed open a door on the landing and led the way into a large, airy bedroom overlooking the back garden.

Alice's gaze settled on the king-size bed and she swallowed. She would share that with Cameron. A shivery feeling swept through her and she turned away, trying to focus on anything except the bed.

A lacy bassinet rested on a stand in the corner with a baby changing table underneath the window. This was a dream come true.

"This is lovely. Thank you so much for everything. I don't have much for Sami, so the baby things are a godsend." Alice laid Sami on the bed, her shoulder aching from all the carrying.

"Radley warned me you wouldn't have much with you." Olivia pulled out some drawers on the changing unit to reveal baby clothes. "These are newborn size so they should fit him. Emma is nine months now. We grew out of them awhile ago, didn't we, my big girl." She kissed her daughter's forehead, then turned and indicated some women's clothes folded on the chair. "I hope these will tide you over until you have a chance to pick up your own things."

Tears pricked Alice's eyes. Cameron's relatives were so kind. She didn't deserve it.

\*\*\*

Cameron passed the ball to George, taking care not to kick too hard. His son ran after it and knocked it on to Radley. This was almost like old times—he and Radley knocking a ball around together in the back garden. Only time had marched on and things had changed so much he barely remembered the carefree boy he had been back then.

George tripped and was straight back up, chasing after the ball, grass stains on his knees. He was such a bright, brave little boy, a credit to Olivia and Radley. He might carry Cameron's genes but Radley was George's father in every way that mattered.

The familiar blend of guilt, longing, and resentment stirred in his chest, but faded much faster than usual. This visit he was simply pleased to see how happy his son was. Many times he had wished he'd been a father to George, but that would have meant marrying Olivia. She was a beautiful woman and a wonderful mother, but not right for him.

You would never catch Olivia doing something daring like working with nomads in the desert as Alice had. Not many young women would. He admired Alice's courage and willingness to take risks to help others. He understood it.

He passed the ball to George and glanced up at the back of Radley's house, at the bedroom windows. Alice was up there with Sami. *His wife and adopted son.* The thought sent a flash of warmth and satisfaction through him. He had a chance to prove to his parents he was not still the irresponsible, selfish son who shirked his responsibilities. Alice and Sami needed him in a way he understood and could help with.

"Hey, Rad. Think I should go up and make sure Alice and Sami have everything they need."

His brother kicked the ball farther away and George dashed after it, his little legs pumping as if he were in a race. Radley came closer. "Your news surprised me. It was a bit sudden between you and Alice. You've only known each other a few weeks."

"It only took you a few weeks to fall in love with Olivia."

Radley nodded thoughtfully. "Point taken. But we didn't marry straight away."

When Radley gave him an is-there-something-you're-not-telling-me look, Cameron glanced down. His brother had always been too perceptive.

"You know how everything seems different in a conflict zone, more urgent." He didn't want to tell his brother he had only married Alice so they could adopt Sami. He wanted his relatives to treat Alice and Sami as though they were really part of the family. Being a husband and father roused his protective instincts. He liked that they needed him. For the first time he understood why Radley was so devoted to his family.

George dashed back, the ball hugged to his chest. Radley gave his son a wry smile. "You're supposed to dribble the ball back with your feet, pal. Picking it up is against the rules."

"You kicked it too far away, Daddy."

Both men chuckled.

George tossed the ball at Cameron's feet. "Play with me, Uncle Cam."

Cameron crouched down to the boy's level. "I need to go inside and see Alice and Sami. You haven't said hello to them yet, but you'll see them later. Sami's very tiny; he's only a few weeks old." He wanted George to like Sami and Alice. He wanted a photo of George holding Sami to keep on his mobile phone.

"Will you play with me some more later?"

"Sure thing." Cameron ran a hand over George's head of thick dark hair, so like his own, and rose to his feet.

He headed inside, a flutter of nerves in his belly. He hadn't been nervous around a woman for years, yet the moment he'd married Alice he'd started feeling like a teenager trying to summon the courage to ask a girl out. Crazy, when she was his wife.

He sat on the second stair, pulled off his boots, then climbed to the next floor. One of the bedroom doors stood open. Inside, Olivia cooed softly to a baby.

"Hey, Livi, which room am I staying in?" he asked.

"This one. Come in." She had a bottle in her hand and leaned over a white lacy bassinet smiling at Sami. "I sent Alice to shower and change. I was going to feed Sami but I really need to go downstairs and get on with preparing dinner." She held out the bottle.

Cameron had watched Alice feed Sami numerous times, but had never done so himself. "Okay, I can do that." He put the bottle on a table beside an easy chair and picked up the tiny boy, now dressed in a blue all-in-one suit with little yellow ducks on it. "Hey there, Sami. You hungry, bud?"

Under Olivia's watchful gaze, he sat with Sami cradled in his arm and put the nipple in the baby's mouth. A smile stretched his lips as the baby latched on and sucked hard.

"Boy, he's hungry," Olivia said with a laugh.

"He always is." Cameron grinned down at the baby, pride swelling inside him. Sami was his son now, his responsibility. It was a great feeling.

He barely noticed Olivia leave the room he was so busy watching Sami, his tiny hands flexing as he sucked.

"You're a good boy, Samikins. I like your ducky romper suit. You look real cute, you know. I bet Alice thinks you're cute as well."

"You both look cute together." He was so engrossed in the baby, Alice startled him.

His gaze jumped to the doorway. Alice's damp blonde hair tumbled over her shoulders, a fluffy white towel wrapped around her body. Her eyes were so blue against her tanned skin. She appeared beautiful and fragile, her cast covered in a plastic wrap. It was hard to believe this was the same woman he'd found in the desert.

Sami finished his bottle and released the nipple. Cameron shifted the baby to his shoulder and rubbed his back to burp him. "I wanted to make sure you had everything you need," he said, glancing away from Alice, suddenly aware she wore only a towel and he'd been staring.

"Olivia loaned me some clothes. Trouble is, she's about six inches taller than me." She sat on the end of the bed and rested her cast on her knees.

"I better get out of here. I expect you want to get dressed." In the hospital, Cameron knew exactly what he was supposed to do. He had a purpose. Here he was uncertain how to treat Alice.

"That's okay. I can wait a few minutes. It's good to see you feeding Sami. I'd like you to spend more time with him."

"You would?" Cameron was surprised. He always got the impression Alice wanted Sami all to herself.

"Yes, it's good for him to get used to a man. He must sense we're different."

"I guess." Cameron finished burping Sami and laid him gently in his bassinet.

Water from Alice's wet hair dripped down her shoulders. She grabbed a folded towel off the end of the bed and tried to dry her hair one-handed.

"Let me."

"Let you what?"

"Dry your hair."

Alice's eyes widened but when he reached for the towel, she released it. He sat on the bed beside her. She turned and he gathered the long blonde strands into the towel and rubbed, moving up to massage her scalp dry with the soft fabric.

Gradually her shoulders relaxed. Her breath hissed out on a sigh of pleasure. The room fell silent except for Sami's soft exhalations and the occasional sound of voices in the garden. After the busy field hospital, it seemed strange being alone together in a private room where nobody would intrude on them.

The side of Cameron's little finger brushed Alice's shoulder. He repeated the move, enjoying the contact with her smooth, warm skin. Long after he had done the job, he continued stroking her head with the towel, inhaling the floral fragrance of her hair.

"You're tense. Let me help you relax," he whispered, his voice gruff.

The wet towel hit the floor and he gathered the damp strands of her hair aside to massage her neck and shoulders. He wanted to touch her, to help her relax, to hear her breath rush out as his fingers stroked her skin.

He wanted this to be a real marriage.

# Chapter Seven

Alice's eyelids drifted down as Cameron's fingers worked magic on her weary muscles. Heat tingled through her and warmed her skin.

She should stop him. It was one thing letting him dry her hair. A massage was another matter. Yet she couldn't bring herself to murmur a word when his touch made her melt inside.

Was he really only being kind, helping her relax because her arm was in a cast? She might almost think he was enjoying this. Yet she wouldn't ask in case she made a fool of herself.

"I've been thinking," he said.

"Aha." Her murmur came out soft and throaty.

"I think you might be stuck with me for longer than you intended."

She frowned, her thoughts chasing around, trying to make sense of things in her hazy, pleasure-filled mind. "What do you mean?"

"We need to stay married until the adoption is ratified over here. I'm the one who signed the adoption papers in Sami's country of birth."

His words jerked Alice back to the moment. She opened her eyes and stared at the white lacy bassinet. He was right. In her mind, she had adopted Sami, but Cameron's signature was on the forms not hers.

65

All her youth her father had tried to control her by taking away the things she wanted or needed. One day he had locked up all her shoes so she couldn't go out. Defiantly, she'd gone out barefoot to show him she wouldn't be controlled like her mother.

Once she left home, she intended to never get in the position where a man had power over her that way. Now Cameron held control of the most precious thing in her life. She bit her lip, the pleasure of his touch fading.

With a flash of disquiet, she rose to her feet. "Thanks. That did help." Her brisk tone sounded anything but grateful.

"You don't need to worry. I won't let you down. I know how important Sami is to you. Together we'll make sure you get to keep him." He firmed his lips, his expression determined.

Was she worrying over nothing? Cameron had been helpful and dependable so far. She had no reason to think he would let her down now. He had already gone far beyond the call of duty by marrying her in the first place. He was nothing like her father.

"So we need to stay married until the adoption is finalized," she said. "That might take six months."

Cameron nodded. "Longer probably." Uncertainty flashed across his face.

Did he regret being tied to her for so long? Perhaps he would miss having a girlfriend?

"Is it going to be a problem for you, being married to me?"

He frowned.

She wasn't making herself clear. Alice sucked in a breath and tried again. "I don't want our arrangement to restrict you. If you want to go out on dates, you should."

His brows drew down in obvious annoyance. "That hasn't even occurred to me."

"Okay." Alice chewed her finger. Something was definitely troubling him. If it wasn't that, she had no idea what was on his mind. "I'm happy to keep pretending for as long as it takes to make the adoption legal."

"Do we have to pretend?"

Now she was confused again. Had he changed his mind? "So you do want an annulment?" she asked tentatively.

His breath whooshed out in frustration. "No. I want to give the marriage a shot. Make it real."

"Real!" Alice's voice came out as a squeak.

Cameron's beautifully sculpted lips flattened with displeasure. "Is that such a terrible suggestion?"

"Not terrible. No. Of course not." Surprising, though.

He rose to his feet in front of her, and his hands settled on either side of her waist.

"If we're going to make this real, we need to get to know each other properly." His fingers lifted to raise her chin. She looked up into the warm depths of his brown eyes, and the breath stalled in her throat.

"Who knows," he said, his voice husky and soft. "We might find we're good together."

Then he leaned down and pressed his firm, warm lips against hers.

Alice walked slowly down the stairs, the handle of Sami's carry seat in her good hand. The rumble of male voices from the kitchen sent a flash of nerves through her.

She hadn't seen Cameron since the previous evening. She'd wound herself in knots of anticipation as bedtime approached, expecting him to sleep in the bed with her. Then after dinner he had announced he needed to visit his lodgings to get his belongings. As it was late he would sleep there and return this morning.

He was obviously back.

She put down Sami's seat, checked her face in the hall mirror, and smoothed creases from the green dress Olivia had loaned her. It was baggy around the bust and too long. The weight had dropped off Alice during her work with the nomads. Half the time she'd had a bad stomach. When she didn't, the food was less than appealing. They ate all parts of an animal including the brain, eyes, feet, and other unmentionable bits that she just couldn't bring herself to eat.

The trouble was she'd always had a boyish figure; now she had barely any shape. Certainly not the sort of womanly curves a man liked. At least the bruises on her face had faded and her nose had returned to normal size.

Male laughter burst from the kitchen, and her heart stuttered. She picked up Sami's carry seat and headed down the hallway. She was comfortable with Cameron when she wasn't worrying about the sleeping arrangements, and Radley seemed like a nice guy. What strummed Alice's nerves was the thought of meeting Cameron's father. A powerful man like Major General Knight would surely be out of the same mold as her father. For men like that, dominating women came as second nature.

Pasting on a smile, she walked into the kitchen, her gaze immediately drawn to Cameron. He sat at the table with George on his lap. They both stared at the screen of a tablet device, obviously engrossed in a game.

"Morning, Alice. How did you sleep?" Olivia's jaunty greeting meant Alice had to drag her attention away from Cameron.

"Very well, thank you. It was pure luxury to sleep in a proper bed."

Radley also sat at the table, Emma beside him in a high chair. He spooned fruit puree into the pretty little girl's open mouth.

"She's like a baby bird." Olivia laughed. "At least our children eat well."

Alice only half listened, distracted as her gaze strayed back to Cameron. He kissed the top of George's head and ruffled his hair. He plainly adored the boy and she could see why. Bright as a button and sweet natured, George looked up and grinned at her. He looked so much like Cameron, but that wasn't surprising as Cameron and Radley were so alike.

Cameron lifted George, stood, and placed the child back on the chair he'd vacated. He rounded the table, relieved her of Sami's chair, and set the baby carrier on the table. Faded denim jeans clung to Cameron's hips and he wore a striped dress shirt with the sleeves folded up to the elbows. It was the first time she had ever seen him out of army uniform. She liked what she saw.

He took her hand and stepped closer, lowering his mouth to her ear. "Sorry for deserting you last night. Was everything all right with Sami?"

His warm breath sent a shivery sensation racing through her. Distracted, it took her a moment to gather her thoughts to answer.

"All fine. Sami got me up about six for a bottle. He'll be ready for another soon, I guess."

Cameron turned and leaned over the baby carrier, wiggling his finger in Sami's palm until the baby gripped his digit. "Hey, little man, you hungry again?" He cast an amused glance at Alice as Sami wedged his fist in his mouth and started sucking.

"The rate he's going he'll double his weight in no time," Alice quipped, trying to ignore the thumping of her heart. Cameron still held her hand, his fingers absently stroking her palm. Part of her wished he would let go so she could think.

He dropped her hand and she immediately missed

his touch. She should be careful what she wished for.

"My turn to feed him, I think." Cameron headed for the bottle sterilizer to prepare the baby's milk.

"Sit down and have some breakfast." Olivia pushed boxes of cereal nearer Alice's place setting on the table. "We've all eaten. I hope you don't mind that we didn't wait. I needed to get on with preparing lunch. Radley's parents will arrive soon."

Alice had just poured some muesli in a bowl and added milk. At the thought of meeting Radley and Cameron's parents, her appetite deserted her.

"Don't worry, they won't bite," Radley said, obviously catching her expression.

"Mum will love Sami," Cameron added, coming back with a full baby bottle. He lifted Sami and sat with the baby cradled in his arm and put the nipple in his mouth.

"Sandra and George are really nice." Olivia placed a rack of toast in front of Alice with some butter and spreads. "They both love children."

She met Cameron's reassuring gaze. Her nerves abated but didn't go away. His relatives had welcomed her, but it was impossible to shake off her fear. Growing up with her father had conditioned her to expect the worst of men. Cameron had shown her some men were considerate and trustworthy. But older men, men in positions of authority and power, still made her wary.

"Hello. We're here." A woman's voice from the hallway made Alice turn from the salad she prepared at the kitchen counter, while Olivia finished up the beef burgers and chicken kebabs for their celebratory barbecue.

"That's Sandra, Cameron's mother," Olivia said, grabbing a tea towel to wipe her hands.

Alice followed Olivia out the kitchen door and halted

beside the stairs. An attractive older woman in a floral sundress and sandals with dark hair and glasses turned to greet Cameron as he came out of the games room, where the boys had been playing snooker.

Ordinary in a nice way, she was relaxed and confident without being too primped. Unlike Alice's mother who either resembled a fashion model or a train wreck.

"Cameron, darling, it's so good to have you home in one piece." His mother threw her arms around him and hugged tightly, then took half a step back and examined him critically, smoothing her hand across his cheek. "You're very tanned."

"It's hot there, Mum."

"I know. I hope you're careful not to overdo the sun."

Cameron and Radley exchanged long-suffering looks, and he squeezed his mother's shoulders. "I'm old enough to look after myself now, you know."

"You'll always be my little boy. I worry about you."

She turned as George raced out of the room, and scooped him up. "How's the birthday boy?"

"Have you got me a birthday present, Grandma?"

Glancing over her shoulder, Sandra checked the open front door. "Granddad will bring it in when he's finished fiddling with the car. He thought he heard a noise in the engine, so goodness knows how long he'll have his head under the hood. Not that he has a clue what he's looking at. Engines have never been his thing." The casual way Sandra talked about her husband gave Alice goose bumps. Her mother wouldn't dream of criticizing her father in front of others.

Sandra hugged Radley next, patting his cheek affectionately, then it was Olivia's turn for a kiss. Alice waited in the shadows beside the stairs, poignant emotions filling her. This was the sort of family life she had dreamed of when she was a little girl.

"Where's my little sweetie girl?" Sandra glanced around.

"Emma's napping," Olivia said. "I'll get her up in a few minutes."

Sandra's curious gaze found Alice, clearly surprised to see a stranger. "Hello, there."

"Hello, Mrs. Knight. It's lovely to meet you."

Cameron threaded his way through the group to Alice's side and put his arm around her waist. "Mum, this is Alice Conway, the woman who rescued the baby."

"Oh, my goodness, George mentioned he arranged an emergency visa for an injured newborn. You're very welcome here, Alice. I can only imagine how terrifying it must be over there." Her gaze settled on the cast covering Alice's arm. "I admire you for being so brave." She stepped forward and kissed Alice's cheek.

Alice returned the brief embrace awkwardly. "Sami wasn't injured. He just has a cleft lip. Cameron says it's easily fixed."

"Over here it's routine. Do you have the little one with you?" Sandra's eyes gleamed in anticipation.

"He's in the kitchen."

Before Alice could say more, Sandra hurried down the hall. Alice followed, the rest of the family on her heels.

"Oh, he's a darling," Sandra exclaimed, leaning over the baby seat.

Sami's intelligent brown eyes tracked the movement of the people crowding around him. He flapped his arms and kicked his legs, grunting with excitement.

"Would you like to hold him?" Alice asked, already unfastening her baby from his seat, sure of Sandra's answer.

"Absolutely." Sandra lifted Sami against her chest and rocked him gently. "You are adorable. Do you know that, little one?" She glanced up. "Did you say his name is Sami?"

Alice nodded. Sandra was such an easy person to talk to and be around. The nerves that had plagued Alice all morning faded.

"I adopted him." Alice's love for Sami bubbled up, making her grin. Sandra would understand her feelings. "He's such a good little boy. I can't believe how lucky I am to have been there in the right place at the right time to save him."

Cameron moved to her side and she grasped his hand enthusiastically. "Cameron was wonderful. I don't know what I'd have done without him."

Cameron's arm slid around her waist and she leaned into him, basking in the warm glow of this close, loving family.

"Actually," Cameron said softly, "we both adopted Sami."

Sandra's brows gathered. "Both of you?"

"Alice and I are married, Mum."

Sandra froze, her expression morphing from shock to surprise before a smile touched her lips. She glanced down at the baby in her arms, her eyes sparkling with pleasure. "Oh, that means Sami is my grandson."

A man cleared his throat, snapping Alice's gaze to the doorway.

"You're married?" The man looked like an older version of Cameron and Radley, tall and distinguished, his dark hair silvered at the temples.

His expression was carefully blank, leaving her unsure of his reaction.

"Yes, a few days ago." Cameron led Alice to his father and the two men embraced. "Alice, this is my father, George Knight. Dad, this is my wife, Alice."

She couldn't imagine *ever* calling this man by his Christian name. "Pleased to meet you." Her voice came out as little more than a whisper. Everyone had stopped talking to watch them. Cameron's father shook her hand, his grip firm, his hand so big hers disappeared.

"This seems rather hasty, Cameron."

Cameron's father disapproved. Alice dared not look him in the face. Instead she stared at the buttons on his jacket, her belly clenching in a horribly familiar way.

"It was the right thing for us," Cameron said.

"Where do you come from, Alice?"

"London." She felt like a naughty student called up in front of the headmaster.

"What does your father do?" That was exactly the sort of question her father would ask when surely he should be more interested in what she did.

"I work for the charity Safe Cradle." She risked a glance at his face and caught his slight smile as he noted she hadn't answered him.

"Yes, I know that. You're the young lady who rescued the baby."

Heat stung Alice's cheeks. Of course, Cameron's dad had been the one to arrange the visa for Sami. Maybe she was looking for a snub when none was intended.

"My father's a High Court judge."

"That's interesting. What's his name? I might know him."

Disquiet whispered through Alice. Her father had nothing to do with her life now. That was how she wanted it to stay.

"Sir Alistair Conway," she offered reluctantly.

"Ah, yes. I am acquainted with him. We were at Oxford together."

Alice's gaze shot up to the man's face in horror. This was terrible. What if he told her father about Sami?

# Chapter Eight

Cameron sealed the tapes on Sami's clean diaper, wiped his hands, and lifted the baby into his arms. He smiled down at the little guy and pressed his lips to the top of his head, breathing in his sweet baby smell. Alice's floral fragrance clung to the baby's hair as well.

"You smell so good I could eat you all up." Laying Sami on the bed, he blew on the baby's chubby tummy, making him kick his legs. Sami's brown gaze followed him with interest as he dressed him in a sleep suit.

Sami gurgled and his little mouth curved at the corners. His first smile! A burst of warm, protective feelings stole Cameron's breath. He lifted Sami into his arms and held him as tightly as he dared, rocking him back and forth. He loved this little boy so much it nearly overwhelmed him.

He loved George too, but this was different. George might be his biological son, but he had never been his to care for and protect. Not like Sami.

"Are you having a cuddle?" Alice wandered in from the bathroom.

"He smiled at me." Cameron's voice came out all choked up, and he cleared his throat.

"Really?" Alice pressed her face against his shoulder to look in Sami's face. "What a clever boy. Are you going to smile for me too?"

The baby yawned hugely and blinked. Cameron and Alice both chuckled, their eyes meeting over the baby's head. Another burst of feeling rocked through Cameron. Something about Alice touched him in a way he'd never experienced before. Was he falling in love with her?

He'd missed her last night, but he'd had to stay away. If they'd slept in the same bed he might have taken things too fast. He needed to give her space to get used to the idea of making this a proper marriage.

But he was done being a gentleman. One night would have to be enough space. Tonight he wanted to share his wife's bed.

"Do you want to give Sami his bottle?" he asked.

"Yes, just let me brush my hair."

Cameron rocked Sami in his arms, humming a nursery rhyme while Alice sat on the padded stool and picked up a hairbrush. She swept the bristles through the long golden strands falling around her shoulders, gleaming like silk in the low lighting.

His hand flexed, imagining the feel of her hair running through his fingers. Her beautiful golden hair had been the first thing he'd noticed about her when he rushed to her aid after she went down. That first time he saw her out in the desert felt like a different lifetime now.

Thank you, God, for throwing this woman in my path, he thought. Sami wriggled and Cameron circled his palm soothingly on the baby's back. Thank you for giving me a second chance to be a good dad as well.

This time he would put his heart and soul into caring for his baby and do the job properly.

Alice stood and slipped off the dressing gown Olivia had loaned her. The cream silk nightdress clung to her skin, still damp from her shower. Acutely aware of Cameron's gaze following her, she fumbled in a drawer for something, but she couldn't remember what.

"I'll take you into London tomorrow to pick up your things from that place you left them."

"The women's refuge. Are you sure you want to come?"

"No way are you going to that rough part of London on your own."

Did he really care about her as much as he seemed to? She couldn't believe it.

Excitement and nerves twisted and tangled inside her as she slid between the crisp sheets and arranged a pillow on her lap so she could lay Sami at the right angle to feed him.

"Here you are. One hungry little boy." Cameron gently settled Sami in the crook of her cast on the pillow and handed her the bottle. Sami's eyes drifted closed, but as soon as the nipple touched his lips he sucked it in and gulped down his milk.

Concentrating on her baby, Alice tried to ignore Cameron as he moved around the room, tidying up baby things. He kicked off his shoes and socks and started unbuttoning his shirt.

Alice struggled to breathe normally, her heart thumping, her skin tingling. What did he expect of her tonight?

"I'm just going to the bathroom."

Alice's gaze rose to Cameron's naked chest, his muscles sculpted with light and shadow by the table lights. He stood at the bottom of the bed, a toothbrush in his hand, and faded denim jeans riding low on his hips. Her breath rushed out in a strange little whimper. His eyebrows rose so she pretended to cough.

When the door closed behind him, she pulled the empty bottle from Sami's mouth and pressed a hand over her eyes. Cameron hadn't even climbed in bed yet and she had already made a fool of herself. She burped Sami and gathered the sleepy baby up to settle him in his bassinet.

Then she turned off all the lights except the one on Cameron's nightstand and lay down. Her breath sounded unusually loud in the stillness of the room as she waited.

He entered softly and bent over the bassinet to kiss Sami before he moved around the bed. Slipping off his jeans, he slid beneath the sheets wearing his underwear.

Alice lay stiffly on her back, sleep about as far from her mind as it was possible to get. She had never felt more awake, or more aware of Cameron, mere inches away from her in the bed. He slid closer, propping his head on his hand. "You're okay with this arrangement, aren't you?"

"Yes."

She rolled onto her side to face him, her pulse racing. She still couldn't believe he was attracted to her. Maybe he just thought they should try to make a go of the marriage for Sami's sake. Alice's teeth worried at her lip.

They stared at each other in the semidarkness, the small bedside light silhouetting Cameron, making it difficult to see his face. That actually made it easier to talk frankly. "I don't understand why you wanted this," Alice said.

"I didn't plan it." Cameron's fingertips brushed the hair back from her face, and lingered on her bare shoulder. "It seems like the right thing to do for you and Sami."

The small bud of hope inside her shriveled. His being here with her was due to his sense of duty.

"If you'd rather date someone else then I won't make a fuss. We only got together for Sami. I never expected you to give up your social life for me."

Cameron gave a wry laugh. "I don't have much of a social life."

"I guess not while you're deployed in a conflict zone, but surely when you come home on leave you must date."

"Yes," he said, reaching out and cupping the back of her head, drawing her closer. "I'm dating my wife. I want *you*, Alice. Not some other woman." Shivers of sensation flowed through her as he leaned closer.

He kissed the tip of her nose, her cheeks, her eyelids, then put his lips against her ear. "Now stop trying to talk me out of how I feel and kiss me, Mrs. Knight."

Alice barely noticed the London streets passing the window of the 4x4 as Cameron drove Radley's car towards the women's refuge to collect her stuff.

She was in love—something she had never thought possible. This wonderful man had swept her off her feet with his soft caresses and gentle lovemaking. She'd had no idea a relationship between a man and woman could be this way. For the first time she understood what people meant when they said they were walking on clouds. She felt both dreamy and excited at the same time.

The GPS directed Cameron to turn right. He swung the large vehicle through the traffic, a frown creasing his brow. "Is this the right way, love? It looks dodgy around here."

"This is where women need the refuge most." Not all women, of course. Some, like her mother, lived in expensive, fashionable parts of town. It didn't mean they didn't need help.

"We're nearly there. Find a space on the edge of the road if you can," she said.

Cameron parallel parked beside a parking meter and cut the engine. He climbed out and came around to open the door for her.

"The refuge is around the corner." She threaded her fingers through his as he took her hand.

They walked past an empty lot littered with trash. Obscene graffiti covered a wall beside the railway line and dirt filled every crack. The area had always been scruffy, but it had deteriorated further.

They turned a corner onto a street of run-down houses. "It's number sixty-two."

A few people gathered around a man hammering on a door, shouting abuse.

"Not that place, I hope?" Cameron halted, keeping a tight grip on her hand.

"Yes. The man's wife is probably inside."

Cameron turned, pulling her with him. "Come on, let's go back to the car."

"No. I want to get my things. Wait a few minutes. Maeve, who runs the place, will have called the police."

Cameron hesitated, his lips pressed in a hard line. "Okay, but if the situation gets worse, we walk away, all right?"

Cameron really did not want to be here, but even more he didn't want Alice here. Thank goodness they hadn't brought Sami. They retreated to stand by a wall covered in graffiti. He tightened his grip on Alice's hand, keeping watch all around. Some of the houses had boarded-up windows and litter lay everywhere.

A siren cut through the air. A few minutes later a police car turned down the road and stopped outside the women's refuge. Two officers jumped out and tried to talk to the man hammering on the door. He stumbled down the steps and took a swing at one of them. They cuffed him, pushed him in the back of their car, and drove off.

Cameron couldn't believe it. "Don't the police take statements from anyone when this happens?"

"Not unless the woman inside files a complaint. They'll lock him up until he's sober and then release him."

Cameron shook his head. This was a different world from the one he lived in. He slipped his arm around her and hurried along the edge of the road, his gaze darting everywhere. "I can't believe you used to work here." He certainly wasn't going to let her work here again.

"Somebody has to help these women."

"I know, love." But it wasn't going to be her. They could argue about it later if necessary. Right now he wanted to get her in and out as quickly as possible. By the time they got back to Radley's expensive car, it would probably be stripped down.

As they neared the house, Alice waved to a woman with a mass of red hair, leaning out of the upper floor window. "Maeve, it's me."

"Alice! I'll be straight down." A few minutes later the front door opened. "I thought you were in a desert somewhere. Come here and give me a hug."

Alice walked into Maeve's open arms. "It's good to see you. I missed you."

"What the hell happened to your arm, darling?" Maeve's gaze rose from Alice's cast and raked over Cameron.

He bristled at the accusation in her eyes.

Alice hugged closer to his side, defusing his indignation with her warm smile. "I was injured in Africa. This is the man who saved me. He's an army doctor, Maj. Cameron Knight. My husband."

Maeve's eyebrows shot up and disappeared in the unruly mop of red hair. A gamut of emotions crossed her face as she assessed him. Finally she held out a hand. "Maeve Brown. I run this place."

"Good to meet you, Maeve." He would forgive this woman for jumping to conclusions. She seemed to be important to Alice. "We saw the altercation at the door. Are you all okay inside?"

A woman's cry distracted Maeve, and she glanced over her shoulder. "Not really. That guy's wife is in a bad way, but she won't let me call an ambulance." She heaved a frustrated sigh. "She won't talk to the police either."

"Would you like me to examine her?" Cameron offered the olive branch, fully expecting her to turn him down.

Maeve's gaze moved back to him, her expression wary. Long moments passed, then she stepped aside. "Yeah, Nina needs a doctor."

A threadbare hall carpet covered the floorboards, but the walls were a cheerful yellow decorated with children's artwork. The smell of pizza drifted from the end of the corridor. Maeve led them to a room at the back that held a couple of beds. A woman in jeans, socks, and a gray T-shirt lay in a fetal position, groaning.

"Kids?" Alice asked under her breath.

"Three in the playroom."

Alice nodded and squeezed Cameron's arm. "See you in a minute."

He watched her slip from the room then turned his full attention on his patient.

"Nina, here's a doctor to see you," Maeve said.

The woman didn't respond. Not a good sign.

Cameron moved to the side of the bed. "Hello, Nina, I'm Dr. Knight. Maeve asked me to take a look at where you're hurt." He lifted aside the woman's long dark hair to see her face. She had a swollen lip and bruising on the side of her face—nothing to account for this degree of discomfort.

She lay with her knees bent and her hands over her belly.

"Nina, I need you to turn onto your back." He glanced at Maeve and she nodded.

After what the woman must have gone through at the hands of her husband, it was best if Cameron touched her as little as possible. He stepped away as

Maeve soothed the woman and coaxed her into rolling over.

"Lift her T-shirt, please," he said.

The sight of angry purple bruising splotched across her belly and ribs sent a sick lurch to Cameron's stomach. He had seen far worse injuries, but never on a woman inflicted by her husband.

Hell. He clenched and released his fist before moving closer to the bed. "I need to palpate the bruised area to check for damage," he said softly to Maeve. "It might be best if you talk to her and reassure her while I undertake the examination."

Maeve nodded and pulled up a chair to sit by Nina's head. She gripped one of her hands and spoke softly. Cameron tuned out the words, only aware of the soothing timbre of her voice. He palpated gently, feeling for damage. A visual inspection suggested possible fractured ribs and he confirmed that diagnosis. He couldn't tell if there was more serious visceral injury inside the chest, but her distress indicated that.

She needed to be admitted to the hospital stat.

He backed away, and Maeve joined him in the hall outside the room. "You need to call for an ambulance immediately. She has fractured ribs and possible internal injuries."

Maeve cursed Nina's husband then hurried away, leaving Cameron alone.

The melodic sound of Alice's voice drew him like a beacon of hope. He pushed open a door to find her kneeling on the floor with three children around her. At the sight of him, the little ones crowded closer to her. The youngest girl, who couldn't be more than two, sat on her knees while the others tucked against her side. Alice put an arm around them and smiled up at him.

"This is Cameron. He's a very kind man who makes sick people better."

He sat on a sagging armchair and the middle girl came over and held out a doll.

"Thank you." He took the doll and cradled it in his arm like he did with Sami. "What's your baby's name?"

"Wendy."

"Just like in Peter Pan." He handed back the doll and the little girl trotted over to Alice and squeezed onto her lap beside her sister, still giving him shy glances.

No obvious bruises showed on the children, but even if the father never physically hurt them, witnessing what happened to their mother would psychologically scar them for life.

Almost silently, the three little girls arranged dolls and soft toys around a square of bright material and set out plastic cups and plates.

He'd seen this before in war zones; children who'd witnessed terrible atrocities would still play. In Afghanistan he'd seen boys kicking a ball about in the street beside the blasted debris of their home, and a little orphan girl with an old brush dressed up as a doll.

It tore his heart out. He'd never imagined he'd feel this way here, in the middle of London.

"Is Mummy all right?" the oldest girl asked Alice.

"She will be. And you'll be safe staying here with Maeve until Mummy is better."

The girl put her arms around Alice's neck and hugged her. The sight of Alice with the three children reminded Cameron of his mother. The realization sideswiped him. Alice loved children just like his mum did. She had that same gentle way about her—somehow soft and feminine but completely determined at the same time.

No wonder he loved her.

# Chapter Nine

It seemed strange to Alice, being back in a military hospital. Although this brand new modern facility near Brize Norton in Oxfordshire was a world away from the decrepit building and makeshift facilities at the field hospital. With its pristine floor tiles and glass walls, the only similarity was that the medical staff wore military uniforms.

Cameron pushed Sami in a stroller borrowed from Olivia. Alice walked at his side, wearing her comfortable old jeans and college sweatshirt, her purse over her shoulder. It was so nice to have her own things back.

The trip to the refuge had been like stepping into her past. A past she'd rather forget. She hadn't realized how different she felt since she met Cameron, as if she finally had a future to look forward to. This life she had with him was a world away from those desperate days when she'd thought she'd never be happy.

"Hi, Cam. You're back." A doctor in uniform stopped.

"Just on leave. This is my wife, Alice, and our son," Cameron said.

Alice smiled and shook the man's hand. Every time they met people Cameron knew, he introduced her and showed off Sami. Any lingering doubt about his commitment to them was quashed by the proud smile on his face.

They climbed in an elevator and headed for the pediatric department on the fourth floor where Lieutenant Colonel Fabian was to meet them. This was the day Alice had been waiting for, Sami's first appointment for his lip.

This hospital was state-of-the-art, with the latest high-tech equipment. The best money could buy to treat wounded military personnel and their families. And the medical staff was first class. Yet nerves tightened her stomach. As they rode the elevator, she fiddled with the edge of her plaster cast, trying to scratch the itching skin underneath. "This darn thing is driving me crazy. When can I have it taken off?"

"Next week." Cameron wrapped an arm around her and kissed her temple. "I'll pop into the orthopedic department before we leave and arrange an appointment for you. It doesn't take long to cut it off."

Alice couldn't wait to have her arm back. She'd be able to hold Sami properly for the first time since he was a newborn.

A computer voice announced the floor number and they stepped out. Sunlight flooded through the huge windows, illuminating the animal pictures that decorated the corridor leading to pediatrics. They followed a trail of animal paw prints and reported to a nurse at the reception desk. "Please take a seat. I'll page Lieutenant Colonel Fabian and tell him you're here."

Sami woke and whimpered, probably sensing his unfamiliar surroundings. Alice leaned over his stroller and stroked his head. "It's all right, Sami sweetie." She glanced up at Cameron. "Perhaps you should lift him out and cuddle him."

"Good idea." Cameron gathered the tiny boy in his arms and walked back and forth, whispering to him and rubbing his back. Frustration filled Alice. She desperately wanted to be able to do that herself, but she couldn't because of her wretched cast. The sooner it was taken off, the better.

"I think he's hungry." Cameron sat beside her and adjusted his grip on Sami so she could see the baby's face. "He's sucking his fist."

"How can he be hungry already? He had a bottle a few minutes before we left. After each bottle, I barely have time to change his diaper and clean up before he's ready for another feed." Not that she had to manage alone. Cameron did more than his share of the work. Olivia helped as well when they needed advice. She had been wonderful.

Cameron rocked Sami in his arms, trying to distract him. "There's Sean Fabian. At least he didn't keep us waiting long."

At Cameron's words, Alice glanced up and did a double take. A tall blond man strode towards them. He had a natural air of authority. Not only that, he was good-looking and he knew it. She could guess he was a high-ranking officer by his confident manner.

Olivia had mentioned his nickname was Lieutenant Colonel Fab because all the nurses were in love with him.

"Cameron, good to see you again." The blond officer held out a hand.

Cameron shifted Sami into one arm to shake. "Morning, Sean. Thanks for fitting us in so quickly."

"Radley tells me you got married, so this must be Mrs. Knight."

"It's Alice," she said, shaking his offered hand. His blue eyes were an extraordinary color, nearly turquoise like the Mediterranean. She'd never seen eyes that color before.

"Please call me Sean." He glanced towards the nurse at reception. "Which consulting room am I in?" From out of nowhere, three nurses appeared and jostled for his attention.

"Let me show you."

"No, I will."

A redhead, obviously the most senior in rank, won out and the other two retreated.

Cameron leaned down and put his lips close to Alice's ear. "Radley says he has to beat them off with a stick."

Alice rolled her eyes and Cameron chuckled.

They followed Sean along a corridor, the winning nurse strutting in front of them, leading the way.

"Here you are, sir. Is there anything else I can do for you, sir?"

"That's all, thank you." To his credit, he hardly gave the woman a second look, his attention on Alice and Cameron.

Reluctantly, the nurse turned away.

"Please come in." Sean ushered them into the consulting room and closed the door. "Do take a seat."

They settled themselves in comfy chairs as he logged in on the computer and read some notes.

"Right, according to Radley, Sami has a left unilateral congenital interruption of the upper lip. Can you hold him up so I can take a look?"

Cameron lifted Sami. Sean examined inside her baby's mouth, and the two men talked in medical jargon for a few minutes. The gist of it seemed to be that Sami's operation would be straightforward.

"Are you happy if we have him in next week?" Sean turned his megawatt smile on Alice.

"Will he need to stay overnight?"

"Normally I'd say yes, but you have Cameron and Radley on hand. If everything goes well, he can come straight home."

Her breath rushed out in relief. She had dreaded her baby spending a night in the hospital. She wanted him at home in his bassinet beside her bed where he belonged.

"Are you okay?" Cameron squeezed her hand. She realized she'd zoned out and the men were waiting for her to answer.

"You're sure he will be all right? There's no risk from the anesthetic or anything like that?"

"As certain as I can be. Nothing is ever one hundred percent safe, but this is a simple procedure. He'll be monitored carefully at all times. You don't need to worry. You can stay with him until he goes into surgery, and see him as soon as he comes out of recovery."

"Can Cameron be in the OR with you?" If she couldn't be with Sami the whole time, she wanted Cameron there to make sure everything was okay.

"We don't allow doctors to operate on members of their own family."

"I'll be with you, love." Cameron's gaze was steady and reassuring. He believed Sami would be fine. Some of Alice's tension faded, but she wouldn't be able to relax completely until her baby boy woke up after his surgery and was well.

"I know this is lousy timing." Olivia shuffled through papers on the kitchen table as she spoke. "The last thing you want the day before Sami's surgery is to be grilled by the people from Adoption Services, but you were lucky to get a date so quickly. Couples usually wait months for their first interview."

Alice nodded, her mind only half-engaged in the conversation. She had tried to prepare for this interview, dressed nicely, and even put on some makeup. Adopting Sami was the most important thing in the world, but how could she concentrate when thoughts of Sami's operation filled her head?

Cameron seemed equally distracted. He finished rolling up the sleeves of his shirt to the elbow, only to immediately roll them down again.

The doorbell rang, jolting through Alice like a clap of thunder. Cameron's gaze jumped to hers. They stared at each other, fear and uncertainty bouncing between them.

Then he smiled, breaking the downward spiral of her emotions. "Come here, sweetheart." He wrapped her in his arms and rocked them both soothingly. "We need to stay positive. We have the foreign adoption papers. We love Sami, and you've been caring for him since he was born. Nobody will look after him better than us. He's our son. This interview is a formality."

Alice pressed her face against his chest, breathing in the herbal fragrance of him that had become so reassuring. "I'm fine," she lied.

She turned to where Sami slept in his stroller and kissed her baby on his forehead for luck. Cameron followed suit. Then they headed to the hall where Olivia's voice sounded as she invited the social workers from the adoption agency inside.

A middle-aged woman with wavy brown hair and glasses and a similarly unremarkable man in a gray suit stepped into the house. "I'm Olivia Knight," she said, shaking their hands. "This is my brother-in-law, Cameron Knight, and his wife, Alice."

Even in her fashionable dress with her hair up, Alice felt gauche beside Olivia in her cream pants and pink cashmere sweater with her glossy dark hair in a chignon. She had the same air of quiet confidence that her husband did.

"I'm Mrs. Sugden." The woman shook Alice's hand and then Cameron's, a warm smile on her face. Some of Alice's tension faded. "This is Mr. Warne, my assistant." The man gave a perfunctory smile and also shook their hands.

Cameron placed a palm on Alice's back. "If you'd like to follow me," he said to their guests. They headed to the dining room as they had planned and seated themselves at the table.

Mrs. Sugden retrieved a file from her briefcase and placed it on the table while Olivia lingered in the doorway.

"Would you like tea or coffee?" Olivia asked. When everyone had answered, she slipped away, leaving the door ajar.

Cameron cleared his throat. "Thank you for coming. We really appreciate how quickly you were able to see us."

"That's no problem, Mr. Knight." Mrs. Sugden flicked through her notes. "I gather this baby is a foreign national you brought into the country. We normally don't condone this without prior approval, but there's a note on the file that the child was in peril."

"Sami needs surgery on his lip. He's going into the hospital tomorrow," Alice said, vocalizing what was uppermost in her mind.

"He'll be fine, love." Cameron's hand covered hers on the polished walnut table. He turned back to the officials. "It's a routine procedure. We have arranged for an eminent surgeon to operate. There's very little risk."

"I'm glad to hear it. Now if we can start by taking down your basic details."

They answered a string of questions until they reached occupation. Olivia brought in a tray of cups and they paused while she handed them out.

"Can you tell me what you do for a living, Mrs. Knight?" the woman asked Alice.

"I've been working for a charity. I plan to stay home and look after Sami now." She glanced at Cameron and he smiled with encouragement. They had discussed this. Both of them wanted Sami to have his mummy at home with him. Cameron earned enough to look after them so Alice had no need to work. Cameron was kind and supportive of her choices. Not like her father who forbade her mother from working for his own reasons.

"That's fine. There's nothing wrong with being a full-time mum if you can afford it. So, what is your occupation?" Both Mrs. Sugden and her assistant switched their attention to Cameron.

"I'm a doctor."

"Excellent." The woman smiled and made a note on her form.

"An army doctor," Cameron continued.

The two social workers glanced at each other, their smiles becoming strained. A tense silence stretched. Alice's breath caught. Something was wrong.

The woman laid down her pen and knitted her fingers over the folder. "Are you aware that when you adopt a child, both parents have to live at home for a minimum of three years to provide a stable family environment?"

A chill swept through Alice. Cameron's hand tightened on hers. "We don't have our own home sorted out yet, but we plan to rent a property close by."

"We can do a home check once you settle in," Mrs. Sugden said. "That's not my concern. The armed forces usually require officers to serve abroad, Mr. Knight. Can you guarantee you won't be deployed away from home for three years?"

"Of course not." A note of frustration crept into Cameron's tone. "I have to go where the army sends me."

"Then I'm sorry. Mr. Knight's occupation will cause a problem."

"You allow single people to adopt." Alice's voice rose as she tried to contain her escalating panic. "How is that different from me looking after Sami on my own while Cameron's away?"

"I assure you it is different. You want to adopt a baby as a couple. Therefore you both need to make the commitment to live with the child for the first three years to establish the family relationship."

"We've already established a family relationship. Sami's been with us since he was born. We're all he knows. He's not going to forget who his daddy is."

Mrs. Sugden closed her folder and put the cap on her pen. "There are rules, I'm afraid."

Cameron abruptly released Alice's hand and rose. "Excuse me a moment." He returned almost immediately with Olivia.

"I'm a lawyer representing Cameron and Alice," she said. "Please explain the problem to me."

Olivia and the adoption officials talked back and forth. Alice tried to listen but the words blurred into a meaningless babble as Olivia fired questions.

A band of pain tightened around Alice's chest. A numb coldness pervaded her body, her thoughts sluggish with fear. She must think of something to say to persuade these people. They couldn't stop her adopting Sami. She was his mum. He was her baby.

"We've already adopted him," she blurted.

"We are aware of the foreign adoption," Mrs. Sugden said. "It still needs to be ratified by a British court to be legal in this country."

"You can't take my baby away. I won't let you."

The cold emptiness inside Alice filled with blistering angry heat. She would not let these heartless morons take Sami. They didn't know her or Cameron. They hadn't even asked to see Sami yet. They didn't care about him. All they cared about were their silly rules, rules enforced in courts by men like her father.

Olivia rounded the table, stood between her and Cameron, and rested her hands on their shoulders. "Keep your cool," she said under her breath. Then louder, "My clients are obviously very upset, Mrs. Sugden. You must understand that Alice rescued Sami from a desperate situation. She saved Sami's life. Since then she has cared for him as her own."

Mrs. Sugden inclined her head and made a note on one of her forms.

"Let's set aside the adoption process and consider the more immediate issue of fostering. Here you have two responsible people with good family support who love this baby. I suggest they are an ideal couple to foster Sami."

Mrs. Sugden glanced at her assistant and nodded. "I see no reason why the baby can't remain with Alice and Cameron for the moment while the adoption process continues. If Mr. Knight leaves the army or can guarantee he will be based in the UK for three years, they stand a good chance of keeping the child."

Mrs. Sugden asked a few more questions. Alice struggled to pull her thoughts together to answer. A storm of emotion wiped her mind, leaving nothing but a mass of exposed nerves. Finally, the adoption officials gathered their things. Cameron rose and showed them to the door.

Alice followed, blinking against tears. If they tried to take Sami, she would leave the country. She'd go back to Africa and live in the desert with him rather than let those people take him away.

She watched as the social workers climbed in their car and drove off.

Cameron pressed his fingers to his temples, pain and frustration clear on his face. "I need to talk to Dad. He'll know what to do."

"Shall I come?" Alice reached for his arm. Right now she wanted to be with him and Sami, to cuddle up together.

Cameron closed his eyes for a few seconds. "No. You stay here, love. I might have to wait for Dad to get home from work. It could make me late."

"I don't mind. I'd rather..." she started, but he wasn't listening.

He hurried towards the kitchen, returning a

moment later with Olivia's car keys. With a perfunctory kiss on her cheek, he stepped out the door, leaving Alice alone in the sudden silence. The tears that had threatened leaked from her eyes and trickled down her cheeks. She rushed almost blindly to the kitchen and bent over Sami's stroller, pressing her face against his dear little body.

Olivia rested a supportive hand on Alice's back. "It'll be all right. I'm on your side and Cameron's parents are solid gold. When I was in trouble a few years ago, Sandra and George stood by me and made sure I was okay. They will help you and Cameron keep Sami. I'm sure of it."

Anger and frustration roiled in Cameron's gut. His fingers clenched so hard on the steering wheel that his hands ached.

"Ignorant, self-important do-gooders," he growled. Who were they to decide he wouldn't be a good father for Sami? The two pen-pushers from the adoption agency had no right to pass judgment on him because he chose to serve in the army and defend his country and the freedoms those two took for granted.

They had no idea what life was like out there where the rules they lived by didn't apply. He'd like to see them running through the desert, being fired on by rebels, trying to save the life of a baby. The baby they now wanted to take away from Alice.

Cameron blew out a breath and consciously tried to relax, tensing and releasing his shoulders and shaking out his hands one after the other. He would not let those people take away the son he and Alice loved. There was always a way to sort things out. His father had a knack for solving problems.

Cameron didn't make a habit of calling on his parents for help. He had always felt they expected him to screw up and need to be bailed out. So he purposely didn't tell them when he got into trouble. But this time was different. This time it affected Sami and Alice.

His foot pressed on the accelerator and the car shot forward from traffic lights, the tires squealing on the road. Anger bubbled up anew as he recalled what Mrs. Sugden had said and the self-righteous smile on her assistant's face as he nodded in agreement.

In what world was it fair for people like that to take away his baby boy over some stupid arbitrary rule? He understood they were trying to make sure adopted children settled into their families, but the authorities should judge each case on its merits. With something as important as adoption, it should never be a one-size-fits-all rule.

Plenty of military wives had babies who only saw their dads during leave. His situation with Sami was no different than that.

He slowed to maneuver the car through the narrow country lanes approaching his childhood home, Willow House, and turned into the gateway. It was nearly six in the evening. His father's car already stood in the drive. He must have just arrived home from work. Stopping, Cameron grabbed the key and jumped out, eager to get inside.

Cameron burst through the front door and hurried along the hall to the kitchen. "Mum, Dad, I need to talk to you."

His mother turned from the counter, an apron around her waist and flour on her fingers. She grabbed a tea towel to wipe her hands, tossing it aside as she reached him. Then she pulled him down into her arms and kissed his cheek. "Cameron, darling, what's the matter? Is somebody hurt?"

"No, everyone's fine. Alice and I had the adoption interview today. They won't let us adopt Sami if I'm posted abroad."

She pulled back, an incredulous look on her face.

"Don't they realize you're in the army?"

"Yes, that's the point. They know I'll be deployed overseas and it's against their rules."

"But military personnel have no say in where they're posted."

"Exactly!"

"Oh, darling." His mother pulled his face down to her shoulder and cupped the back of his head, murmuring to him as though he were a little boy who'd bumped his knee. A fresh burst of frustration at the unfairness of the situation brought tears to his eyes. He swallowed hard and eased out of his mother's embrace to stride back and forth across the room.

"I won't accept this. I promised myself this time I would do the right thing. I won't let them take Sami from Alice. I'll resign from the army and find a job in a civilian hospital if that's what it takes to keep my son."

And he would. But at the thought of leaving the army, something inside him withered. He specialized in front-line trauma care. It was challenging, dangerous, and exhausting, but battlefield medicine was what he did best. On his first deployment in Afghanistan he'd discovered he thrived under extreme conditions. His satisfaction when he saved the life of a soldier who might otherwise have died was off the scale.

But he *would* give that up for Alice and Sami if he had to.

"George, can you come down here?" his mother shouted down the hall. A few minutes later his father's footsteps sounded on the stairs and he hurried into the kitchen.

"What's the problem?"

"The adoption agency won't let Alice and me adopt Sami because I'm in the army."

His father's expression tightened, and his lips thinned.

Cameron repeated what had been said in the

interview earlier.

"I have never heard anything so blatantly unfair or discriminatory against military families. This is totally unacceptable. I'll make damn sure the Ministry of Defense kicks up a stink about it."

"I suppose there's no chance I can stay in the army and request not to be deployed abroad for three years?" Cameron knew his father had power. He wasn't sure how far it went.

His father sat down and ran a hand over his face. "I'd like to say yes but in truth, even I can't guarantee that. We like to think we plan ahead, but we don't have a crystal ball. If a military uprising or regional conflict threatens Western interests, we have to respond. The medical corps are always needed. Anyway, I thought you liked front-line assignments."

"I do."

"I don't," his mother said. "I worry about you. I'm sure Alice will worry as well."

Cameron met his father's gaze and they shared a moment of understanding, man to man. Cameron straightened his spine. The fine balance between doing his duty to the best of his ability, working to his strengths to serve his country, and also taking into account the needs of his family was something new to Cameron. He'd been selfish in the past, putting what he wanted ahead of other responsibilities.

That had been his problem when Olivia gave birth to George. The promise of his exciting career took precedence over his obligation to her. In the past six years, he had grown up. Now he understood a man had to balance his responsibilities. Not an easy task.

"Compromise is the name of the game," his father said softly.

"I tried to do the right thing. Instead I've let Alice and Sami down."

Cameron pinched the bridge of his nose and

dropped into a seat. He'd thought that by marrying Alice he would help a brave young woman adopt the baby she loved. Along the way he had fallen in love with them both. They'd become the most important people in his life.

To think she might have been better off without him ached like a punch in the stomach. The adoption agency might well have approved her as a single mum. Of course he would never know, but Alice must wonder.

His father rose and rested a hand on his shoulder. "There will be a way around this, son. Don't do anything rash like resign from the army. You and Alice hang in there. Give me some time to think of options. I'll do my best for you."

# Chapter Ten

Cameron put his arm around Alice as they walked into the hospital, the handle of Sami's car seat in his other hand. She glanced up at him as they headed to the elevator, but he didn't notice. He stood aside to let her walk in first, then pushed the button for pediatrics. He was doing all the right things but he wasn't really present with her.

On the drive to the hospital, he'd barely said a word. Every time Alice tried to start a conversation about the adoption, Cameron cut her off. "Let's get today over with first," he'd say.

It had been very late when he returned from his parents' house the previous night, but she'd stayed awake, waiting for him. He'd slipped into bed beside her with nothing but a brief greeting. For the first time since they became lovers, he hadn't reached for her.

She had wanted to snuggle up and draw strength from him, share this worry and soothe each other. Isn't that what being married was all about—sharing the problems as well as the joys? Instead he had distanced himself from her.

"Here we are," he said, squeezing her hand as the robotic voice announced their floor. They stepped out into the now familiar corridor of the pediatric department with its colorful walls and large animal pictures designed to make sick children who visited the hospital feel more at home.

Cameron led the way into the reception area and checked in with the nurse. "Lieutenant Colonel Fabian will be right down," she said. "Take a seat for a few minutes, please."

Alice sat and picked at the worn edge of her plaster cast. "It will be so great to get this darned thing off. I can't wait to hold Sami in both arms after the surgery."

Cameron placed a restraining hand over her nervous fingers. "Don't worry, love. Sami will be fine. It's just a routine procedure."

All the Knights had told her this many times. She believed them, yet she still ached at the thought of her baby boy suffering any pain or discomfort. But Sami's surgery wasn't what bothered her most. It was the rest of his life, and where he would spend it that now consumed her thoughts.

She was his mother. How could anyone think of taking him away from her?

These same thoughts had circled in her head all night. She wanted to call Mrs. Sugden and her sidekick and tell them exactly what it had been like in the nomads' camp when the rebels had attacked—the deafening gunfire, the swirling smoke, the reek of blood and other horrible things, the gut-churning fear.

If they knew how terrified she had been when she dashed back to the birthing tent, wrapped Sami and hid him under her jacket, then ran for her life with the three women and their children, all the time expecting a bullet in the back, maybe they would understand how much Sami meant to her.

"Cameron, Alice. Good to see you." Lieutenant Colonel Fabian strode towards them wearing green scrubs that made his Mediterranean eyes appear more green than blue. "How's Sami today?"

"He had a good night," Cameron said.

"He's only six weeks old and he's already sleeping through the night." Alice couldn't resist boasting about how good her baby was.

"I hope I'm as lucky with my children." Sean grinned with obvious pride. "My wife is expecting twins."

"Congratulations, mate." Cameron shook his hand.

"Congratulations. That's wonderful. I bet you're excited," Alice said, trying to pretend she could chat like a normal mum who wasn't terrified the adoption agency would take her baby away.

"Yes, it's certainly going to be a new experience."

"Do you want us to bring Sami through?" Cameron directed them back to the matter at hand.

"Yes, of course. This way."

They followed Sean to a room with a hospital bassinet. While Cameron signed some forms for Sean, a nurse entered and lifted Sami from his carry seat into the crib. She removed his sleep suit and vest, leaving him in his diaper. Then she covered him with clean hospital bedding.

"There, he'll stay nice and warm, don't you worry." She handed Sami's clothes to Alice. "You hold on to those for me. He can have them back on when we're finished."

Cameron wrapped an arm around Alice's waist. "Time to say good-bye to him for a little while."

Even though Alice had promised herself she wouldn't cry, tears flooded her eyes as she leaned into the crib and kissed Sami. "You be a good boy, sweetie. Mummy will be thinking of you the whole time. I'll see you soon."

When she withdrew, Cameron bent down and kissed Sami as well, running a gentle hand over his hair, a tell-tale sheen to his eyes.

"You'll see him in a couple of hours." Sean smiled kindly.

Cameron rested a hand on Alice's back and guided

her to the door. She glanced over her shoulder as they went out to see the nurse wheeling a tray holding medical implements up to Sami's bassinet.

Cameron firmly closed the door.

"What are they going to do to him now?"

"He'll be given a sedative to relax him, then they'll take him down to the OR."

Alice sucked on her lip, her insides churning with many conflicting emotions. She wanted this for Sami, wanted his lip to be repaired, but she couldn't help worrying. Yet she almost welcomed the transient worry about the operation as it pushed aside her greater concerns over the adoption.

"Let's take you down to have your cast removed." Cameron took her hand and they stepped in the elevator and went down a couple of floors. They checked in and within ten minutes Alice was called into a room where a medical technician with a tool that resembled a mini circular saw cut the plaster cast off her arm.

As it fell away, relief burst through her to see her arm back to normal.

"Let me take a look." Cameron lifted her arm and felt up and down the bones in the two places where it had broken. "Straighten for me." He flexed her joints and then smiled. "All looks good."

It was strange to remember Cameron had set her bones before she knew him, when he was just a face behind a clinical mask, a kind pair of brown eyes as she went under the anesthetic.

Wordlessly, she leaned into the firm strength of his chest and encircled his waist with her arms. His arms closed around her, his lips pressing against her temple. The medical technician left the room, closing the door softly behind her.

For long moments they simply held each other, reveling in the simple pleasure of being able to do so.

"Thank you," Alice whispered.

"What for?" he said.

"Everything."

Cameron's chest expanded beneath her cheek as he sucked in a breath. "I'm not sure I've done you much good. I wanted to help, but marrying me probably made life more difficult. You might have been able to adopt him as a single parent. Then you wouldn't have this hassle with the adoption agency."

"I wouldn't have you, either."

Cameron's arms tightened around her. "Would that matter?"

"Of course." Alice pulled back to see Cameron's face, surprised by the vulnerability in his eyes.

"I love you, Cam." And she did, as much as she loved Sami. She didn't want to lose either of them. She pulled his head down and kissed him, enjoying the freedom to touch his back and hair with both hands.

Thank God she had joined the charity and ended up in the desert. Thank God she had been injured. Otherwise she wouldn't have Sami and Cameron in her life.

Cameron kissed her back, stroking his fingers through her hair and pulling her close. "I love you too, Alice. I'll do whatever it takes to make sure they let us adopt Sami, even if I have to leave the army. I won't let you down."

"But the army's your life." Anxiety pulsed through Alice. Cameron had lived and breathed army medicine since he was a child. With his father and brother both army doctors, it was in his blood. He thrived on working in the field hospital. He excelled at it. She'd seen that firsthand.

From the start, she had known he'd be deployed abroad much of the time. She accepted that. She wanted him to be happy and fulfilled.

If he left the army and worked as a doctor in the UK,

they could live together as a family all the time and satisfy the adoption authorities. But would he be happy? Would he always regret losing the life he loved?

The chilly wind cut through Cameron's coat and jeans as he walked out of the woodland into the field. He wrapped an arm around Sami, snug against his chest in a baby carrier, and gripped Alice's gloved hand tighter.

The weekend of George's birthday had been warm and sunny, but as September drew to a close, the weather had turned. It seemed they had gone straight from summer to winter and missed out on autumn.

The weather pattern matched his mood. He'd arrived home happy and full of optimism for the future. Now a cold chill of uncertainty hung over him. In less than a week his leave ended and he must return to Africa. Yet the adoption process was far from resolved. Where Sami was concerned, everything was uncertain.

"Hang on a moment, Cam. I think Sami's dressing's caught on his hood."

Alice stood on her toes and peered at the baby's face where it lay against his chest. Four days after Sami's operation, he was healing nicely. Sean Fabian's stitching was a work of art. Cameron had never seen the like and could never hope to match the lieutenant colonel's skill.

Before they left for their walk Cameron had cleaned the wound, applied antibiotic cream, and redressed it. The only problem was the corner of the sticky tape holding the dressing in place kept catching on things.

"I'll get it." Cameron stroked a finger over his son's cheek and flattened the white tape.

Another blast of chilly wind made Alice shudder and rub her hands together. She tugged the wooly hat Olivia had loaned her farther down over her ears. "I'd forgotten how cold it gets here."

"Come on, let's hurry and go inside."

105

They strode along the worn path across the grassy field towards Henford, the local village. The house they had come to look at was at the edge of the village, the last one in a new development.

The rental property sat on a small, level plot with a square grass backyard. From here Cameron could see the side of the place adjacent to the field.

They reached the hedge beside the road and passed through the small gate at the end of the footpath.

Cameron turned to face the neat two-story brick house with its shiny green front door and brass door knocker. The place was modest in size, a kitchen/dinette, sitting room, and cloakroom downstairs, and two bedrooms and a bathroom upstairs. And it was theirs—or it was for six months until Cameron had time to purchase a home for his family.

That's if the adoption agency approved them and allowed Alice to have Sami. If not, she'd leave the country. Then he didn't know where he'd call home, other than it would be wherever Alice and Sami ended up.

Wrapping his arm around Alice's shoulders, he pulled her close. She was so small and frail inside Olivia's big fleecy coat. He wished she would eat more and put on weight. At twenty-six, she could still pass for eighteen. Her slight build worried him and fired protective instincts that had lain dormant until he met her.

"What do you think of the place?" he asked.

"I like it." She grinned up at him and a strange fluttery sensation filled his chest. He bent and pressed his lips to hers quickly, making her laugh.

"It's only half a mile across the field to Olivia and Radley's house, so you don't need a car," he said. "Although I think you should learn to drive."

She shrugged. "I didn't need to when I lived in

London."

"I know. But now you live in the country you do need to. Olivia offered to teach you to drive, so don't let her forget." Cameron wished he could teach her, but he wouldn't be back again until Christmas.

He sucked in a breath of chilly air and released it slowly. He loved his job. From the moment he'd qualified as a doctor and completed his officer's training at the Royal Military Academy Sandhurst, he had wanted to be posted abroad; the more dangerous the location, the better. He loved the challenge and had always been eager to get back to work after his leave. This was the first time he'd be reluctant to go.

He wished he could stay with Alice and Sami. Radley was lucky his specialty allowed him to be posted to the UK. Wounded service personnel from all over the world were brought to him.

Cameron's specialty could only be practiced on the front line. The nearest alternative was a civilian hospital emergency room. That would be tame in comparison. The army was in his blood. He wanted to save the lives of soldiers, not patch up brawling drunks and soccer hooligans.

Alice pulled a shiny key from her pocket and held it up. "Shall we go inside?"

"Sounds like a plan." He flashed a smile as she pushed the key in the lock and turned. The smell of fresh paint greeted them inside. Although tiny, the place was clean and new.

Alice wandered around, running her fingers along the mantel over the gas fireplace and touching the floral curtains. "When is your furniture arriving?"

"In three days." He'd moved heaven and earth to find a carrier who would ship the stuff from his army lodgings in time for him to move in here with Alice before he had to leave.

She wandered through to the kitchen. Following, he

watched her open cupboards and check the controls on the oven.

"I can imagine you here with Sami." She'd stand Sami's seat on the kitchen counter so he could see out the window while she prepared his bottle.

Alice pulled off her hat, leaned back against the counter, and stared at him. Her blue eyes were so big in her face, her expression pensive and vulnerable. "Can't you imagine yourself here with us?"

"Yes," he said firmly. But he would only have two days with them before he left. Most of the time Alice would be here alone, caring for Sami, trying to sort out the adoption, living her life without him.

A hollow sense of loss filled him as if he had already gone. He caught Alice up and sat her on the counter so they were eye to eye. Then he kissed her and drew her close against him beside Sami.

He'd always rolled his eyes at his mother's tears when his dad went away. Now he understood how she felt.

Alice stood behind Cameron as he changed Sami's diaper, wrapped her arms around his waist, and pressed her cheek to his back. This was the last time he would change Sami for months, the last time she would be able to hug him like this. In thirty minutes he'd be gone.

Pain fisted around her heart. She breathed slowly through her mouth until the urge to cry went away. She had promised herself she would not make a fuss when he left. The army was his job, something very important to him. She didn't want to make him feel bad about leaving.

"Here you are." Cameron turned and passed Sami to her. "I'll just wash my hands, then I can give him a bottle before I go."

Alice wandered out to the tiny landing while the

water ran in the bathroom. She rocked Sami as she descended the stairs, the motion soothing her as much as the baby.

Cameron's footsteps thudded down behind her. He took Sami from her arms and gathered him close again.

"Sit down. I'll bring you the bottle." She had prepared it a few minutes ago, made sure she had everything laid out and ready so he had no interruptions just before he left.

With the bottle in hand, she dropped onto the sofa at his side and snuggled against him, watching her son's mouth as he latched on to the nipple. The nurse had warned that Sami might take a few days to adapt to the change in his lip, and he could have trouble feeding.

That hadn't happened. Sami carried on as though nothing had changed. That was what she must do when Cameron left.

Carry on.

The pain in her chest flared again, leaving her nauseated. "I'll miss you," she whispered.

"I'll miss you too, love. So much." Cameron finished burping Sami and laid him on a baby play mat on the carpet. He pulled Alice onto his lap and held her close, kissing her until they were both out of breath.

She touched the bare third finger of her left hand. He'd never gotten around to buying her an engagement or wedding ring. It wasn't really important, but the oversight made her feel insecure. She had wondered if he was less bothered about the impeding separation than she was. His kiss reassured her.

The doorbell rang. Alice's emotions flared almost out of control. Tears flooded her eyes. She swallowed hard to fight them back.

"That'll be Rad," Cameron said. His brother was dropping him at RAF Brize Norton to catch his flight. "I'd better not keep him waiting."

Alice released him and he kneeled to kiss Sami one

last time. "Be good for Mummy, bud. Daddy will be thinking of you."

Alice knotted her fist in the hem of her oversized T-shirt, struggling for control. She followed Cameron to the front door where his bag lay packed and ready.

Turning, he took her in his arms again, pulling her tight against him. She tried to memorize the sensation of his hard masculine body against hers.

"Remember, you can text me or e-mail me anytime. I won't have my phone with me all the time, but I'll reply as soon as I can."

"Okay."

"Let me know if there are any developments in the adoption saga."

She nodded, unable to answer, sure that if she opened her mouth to speak she would blubber instead.

"If you need anything, Radley and Olivia are just up the road. All right?"

Alice nodded again, her face pressed to Cameron's shirt front. Dressed in his sandy-colored T-shirt, desert combat pants, and boots, the sight brought back memories of the time she spent with him in the field hospital. Good memories.

His fingers found her chin and tilted her face up so he could see her. "I love you, Alice. I'll be home for Christmas. I promise. I have leave booked and Dad will make sure I get it."

He kissed her again, slowly and tenderly, his fingers sliding into her hair. Then he drew back and blew out a breath. He picked up his bag and opened the door.

Alice grabbed his sleeve. "I love you too."

He quickly kissed her once more, then went out and shut the door between them.

Alice stood for a moment, frozen in denial, her stubborn brain refusing to accept he was gone. She hurried back to the sitting room where Sami lay on the floor, and rushed to the window in time to see Radley's big black 4x4 drive away. She caught a glimpse of Cameron in the passenger seat, then the car disappeared from view.

Hot pain exploded in her chest and seared along her nerves.

He'd gone.

He'd ripped out a vital part of her and taken it with him. How had Cameron become so important to her in such a short time?

At least she had his things. The whole house was full of Cameron's possessions: his furniture, his family photographs, his sports trophies. And she loved that. She might not have him, but she was surrounded by the mementos of his life.

He would come back. She just had to be patient.

# Chapter Eleven

The ever present dust tasted gritty in Cameron's mouth as he took his seat in the Merlin helicopter with the other soldiers and two medical technicians.

The captain shouted orders to his men as the chopper took off and headed out over the desert. A patrol vehicle had come under fire and there were casualties.

Cameron's heart thudded as the captain spoke to the pilot and another update on the attack came in.

"There are two men down, Major," the captain said to him. "When we land, you wait for the signal before you exit, please, sir."

Cameron nodded. He followed the safety protocols more closely than he had in the past, and didn't take unnecessary risks. Danger didn't give him the buzz it used to. Now he had more to lose.

He stared down at his hands, let his gaze drift, and pictured Alice and Sami as they'd looked that last morning in bed. He'd made love to Alice, then they'd brought Sami into bed with them for a cuddle before they got up.

Alice and Sami might be a few thousand miles away, but they were always in his heart, affecting everything he thought and everything he did.

The front- and rear-mounted machine guns both

opened fire, the deafening rattle beating against his ear drums in the enclosed space. The firing ceased abruptly, leaving Cameron's ears ringing. He wiped gritty sweat off his upper lip as he leaned forward to peer out of the doors at the landscape below.

"Major Knight, hostile forces are in retreat but there are multiple casualties," a corporal said to him.

A few minutes later the Merlin touched down and the soldiers poured out. The *rat-tat-tat* of gunfire sounded from all directions.

Cameron unbuckled his safety harness and grabbed his medical kit, watching for the signal it was safe for him to jump out. The intermittent gunfire quieted, leaving a tense, eerie silence as hot sandy air blew in the open doorway.

"All clear, sir," the corporal shouted. Cameron paused at the door to survey the area, then dashed out, stones crunching under his boots as he headed for the nearest man down.

An infantryman lay behind a rock with his commanding officer. He was bleeding heavily, his uniform soaked with it, but he still had a gun in his hand.

The officer had multiple fragmentation injury from the blast when an IED took out the Snatch Landrover at the head of the convoy. It had torn through his uniform and caused numerous wounds on his arms and chest, but he wasn't critical. He switched his attention to the other man.

The infantryman dropped his gun, closed his eyes, and flopped back. Cameron pulled open metal closures and ripped apart Velcro to open his jacket, then cut away his T-shirt beneath. When he mopped up the blood, he found two gunshot wounds.

The heat beat down on him. He licked dry lips as he tuned out the shouts of the soldiers and the odd burst of gunfire to concentrate on stabilizing his patient so he could be moved. The two medical technicians brought a stretcher, loaded the man on, and carried him back to the Merlin. He helped load the wounded officer on another stretcher and two of his team took him.

Cameron moved to continue his search for wounded, but the unit captain signaled him back to the helicopter. "The rest are walking wounded and they're already aboard."

Cameron ran back to the helicopter, dumped his medical pack, and crouched to check his patients while the medical technicians treated the less seriously injured. The officer was unconscious but the other man's eyes opened.

"It hurts."

"What's your name?" Cameron asked.

"Hugo."

"Well, Hugo, we're on our way back to Rejerrah now." Cameron squeezed the man's shoulder, trying to hold his attention. He didn't want to give him anything for the pain just yet. They would operate as soon as they reached the hospital. "Hang in there, Hugo. Ten minutes and we'll have you back." There would be a team ready to operate. Once they got an injured man into the OR, his chances of survival were excellent.

Even though he was in acute pain, the soldier fumbled to retrieve something from his pocket. When Cameron realized what he was doing he helped, pulling a photograph out and holding it up for the man to see.

"My wife and daughter." Hugo stared at the picture for a few moments, then his eyelids fell again.

Cameron glanced at the image of a pretty woman with dark hair and a little girl with pigtails. He thanked God that he'd arrived in time to save this man's life. This woman and her daughter would get the man they loved back, but it was a close call.

Cameron missed Alice and Sami every moment, but for the first time since he arrived two weeks ago, he was glad to be here. He did make a difference. He did help people. That's what he wanted to do with his life. When he had a moment, he would call his father and find out if he'd had any ideas about how to handle the adoption authorities. He really did not want to give this up.

Alice pulled away from a road junction in Olivia's car and shifted up through the gears smoothly.

"Wonderful," Olivia said from beside her. "You've picked this up so quickly. You're a natural."

"Thanks. I'd never even tried to drive before." Her father had always told her she didn't need to learn. He had never let her mother learn either.

"You need to go online and book your practical driving test as soon as possible. There might be a waiting list."

Alice nodded. She had passed her written driving test a couple of days ago and had already checked the available dates for the practical. Her aim was to pass before Cameron came home at Christmastime. She wanted to surprise him by picking him up from the airport.

At the thought of Cameron, an ache throbbed inside. It had taken six weeks, but the hollow sense of loss had faded to a bearable level now. They chatted every day by e-mail, text, or on the phone. It allowed her to share with him some of the things that happened and keep him updated on Sami's progress. She made sure to send him a new photo of Sami every day as well.

She was coping. After a few years, the separations would be easier to bear. One day down the line, Cameron would probably be stationed in the UK and they could spend more time together.

"Gosh," Olivia exclaimed. "Look at the time. We've been out for two hours."

"It doesn't feel that long." Alice enjoyed driving. It was a liberating experience being able to get about on her own without needing a bus or train. They had driven all over the place today, through Oxford, along the motorway, down country lanes—all good experience.

"I expect it feels like two hours to my poor husband. He loves the children dearly, and he's very good with them, but he's probably ready for a break."

Alice turned towards Henford, the local village, and threaded her way along the narrower roads back towards Radley and Olivia's house.

Ten minutes later she swung the car between the stone gateposts and crunched up the drive. An expensive new silver sports car was parked outside the front door. Alice pulled up beside it. "Looks like you have visitors."

Olivia frowned as she climbed out. "I don't recognize the car. Maybe it's somebody Radley knows from work."

Alice locked the car and handed the keys to Olivia. "Thank you so much for spending time helping me practice. I really appreciate it." For the last six weeks she'd taken two lessons a week with a driving school, and spent as much time as possible practicing in Olivia's car.

"You're welcome. You're family and the Knights are all about helping family."

Alice had grown to understand that sentiment in the three months she'd been married to Cameron. It was so different from her childhood experience of family. It took a little getting used to, but she liked knowing that whatever happened she was not alone. Even with Cameron thousands of miles away, she had relatives to call on when she needed help.

She followed Olivia inside, her thoughts turning to Sami. She couldn't wait to see her baby boy again. Radley's deep laugh sounded from the sitting room, making Alice smile. So much about Radley reminded her of Cameron. It was a bittersweet thing being around Cameron's older brother.

Then another male voice joined in the laughter. Alice stumbled to a halt.

Her father? He couldn't be here.

She strained her ears to hear the men's voices. Any doubt disappeared as she identified her father's authoritarian tone.

How had he known to find her here? The adoption agency must have told him. That meant he knew about Sami. Her heart lurched, nausea clenching her stomach.

Olivia had already reached the sitting room door. She pushed it open. "Hello, we're back."

"Good timing," Radley said. "Alice's parents have just arrived."

Alice smoothed her hands down the front of her dress, summoning her composure. She would not crawl in there all meek and submissive. Her father had no control over her now. She was twenty-six and a married woman. No way would she let him use Sami to control her.

Head high, Alice strode into the room and halted beside Olivia. "Hello, Dad, Mum, how are you?"

Her mother was stunning in a peach silk dress and matching shoes, her makeup perfect, her blonde hair in a neat chignon.

"Alice, darling." She stepped forward and they kissed each other's cheeks.

Alice's father stood beside Radley, his expression carefully blank. Only someone who knew him well would notice the tell-tale tightness around his mouth. He was furious with her.

"It would have been nice to know you were back in the country," he said.

She hadn't told him she'd left. He must have been keeping tabs on her. Being a High Court judge, he had all sorts of contacts.

"I'm back safely, thank you." She was going to be civil if it killed her.

"We came to meet your husband, but I understand he's out of the country."

"Yes. He's in the army." She stared at her father's forehead. She had learned not to look in his eyes.

"We also want to see this baby you hope to adopt. It seems only fair we should be involved if we're to become its grandparents." A hint of disapproval crept into his tone and a chill went through Alice. This was why he'd come. As far as her father was concerned, the people in his life existed only to serve him or make him look good. Sami had to pass inspection before he qualified.

"Sami's slept most of the time you were out," Radley said. "He might be awake now."

Radley seemed to accept her father at face value, but Olivia was pale and wide-eyed as if she'd seen a ghost. Maybe she'd met Judge Conway in court. He had the reputation for being unpleasant to female legal counsel.

"I'll bring Sami down." Alice might not want to show him to her father, but she was eager for her mother to meet her baby boy.

She left the room, ran up the stairs, and entered the bedroom she and Cameron had shared when they stayed here. Closing the door, she leaned back against it for a few seconds to catch her breath, her heart thumping. She went to Sami's bassinet to find him lying quietly, his intelligent brown eyes tracking a mobile hung from the ceiling. "Hey, baby boy. Were you good for Uncle Radley?"

At the sound of her voice, Sami gurgled and kicked his legs. He'd started to do mini pushups when she laid him on his front on his play mat and he reached for toys now. She lifted him and deposited him on the mat, taking her time changing his diaper.

When he had a clean bottom and there was no other reason to postpone, she gathered him in her arms and walked downstairs, pausing outside the sitting room to listen to her father regaling Radley with stories of when he rowed for Oxford University and won the famous boat race on the River Thames.

He sounded normal when he was with other men. Why did he have to behave like a controlling jerk with his family?

With a sigh, Alice slipped quietly through the door. Her mother rose immediately and came to her. "Oh, he's sweet. What happened to his lip, darling?"

"He had a cleft lip, but it was repaired by a friend of Radley's about six weeks ago. The scar should fade to almost nothing eventually."

"Poor little poppet."

"Considering his uncertain start in life, he's a very laid-back baby." Olivia joined them with Emma in her arms. "I wish my daughter would take a page out of Sami's book."

"Would you like to hold him?" Alice asked her mother.

With a rare impulsive smile, Alice's mother stretched out her hands to accept the baby and cuddled him against the peach silk of her dress. Guilt whispered through Alice. She'd known her mother would love Sami. She should have taken him to see her sooner. But it was a fact of life that her mother could not keep anything from her father. The moment she'd known about Sami, Alistair Conway would also have known.

That was academic now, of course. He knew anyway. She sensed rather than saw her father approach. Her skin prickled, the tiny hairs on her neck raised in warning.

"He's black." Her father's words fell into the room with a thud of disapproval.

"I know." Alice glanced over her shoulder at the

mask of anger on her father's face.

"This is ridiculous. I won't allow you to adopt a black baby."

Alice's protective maternal instinct roused. She gently retrieved her baby from her mother's arms and held him close, cupping his dear little head against her shoulder.

"Cameron and I don't need your permission. For your information, *his* parents are thrilled with Sami."

Her father gave a dismissive grunt. "Your husband isn't even here to speak for himself. No judge will allow an absent parent to adopt. And how do we know you're really married to this man?" He gestured at her bare hand.

"That's enough. I think it's time you left." Radley stepped in front of her father, shielding her and Sami from his view. Alice had wondered how a gentle man like Radley had made colonel so young. Now she got a glimpse of a different side of him as he stood his ground beneath her father's steely gaze.

Alice's mother froze, her obvious distress tearing at Alice's heart. Why didn't she just walk out and leave the man? Alice had tried so hard to help her be strong, yet the one time they'd made it to a women's refuge, her mother had lasted one night before she caved and went home.

Leaning close, Alice kissed her cheek. "I'll call you."

"I'm sorry." She hurried towards the door and Radley stood aside to let her past.

"That child is not for you," Alice's father said. "I'll make sure of it." Then the door slammed and Radley cursed.

The moment they were gone, Alice's bravado collapsed. She sank into the sofa, her muscles trembling.

Her father did not make idle threats.

*\*\**

This was Cameron's favorite time of day. He sat on the hill above the field hospital, staring out across the desert. The sky, an endless expanse of deepest navy speckled with points of light, made him feel he was somewhere magical and out of this world.

The heat of the day had faded and the temperature was more bearable. These first few weeks of November, a cooler wind had replaced the hot gusts that filled his eyes, nose, and mouth with gritty dust. The torrential bursts of rain had stopped and the humidity had fallen. It was a welcome relief from the muggy, baking conditions that left him soaked with sweat, and made his dust-encrusted clothes stick to his skin.

He pulled his mobile phone from his pocket, tapped the screen, and checked the signal strength, then called Alice.

A grin stretched his lips in anticipation of hearing her voice. The last couple of weeks she'd started holding the phone up to Sami's mouth. Sometimes he obliged them and made one of his cute babbling sounds for his dad.

"Hello, Cam." The slight catch in Alice's voice wiped his smile and replaced it with a frown.

"Is anything wrong with Sami?"

"No."

"What's the matter then, love?"

Silence.

He'd learned that she didn't like to bother him with problems. She tried to deal with things herself and pretend all was well.

"Alice, tell me."

"You can't do anything about it."

"I can't if you don't tell me." Of course, if she did tell him he was too far away to help much, but he could always call Radley or his father if the problem was serious. And he sensed this was.

"My father's found out about Sami. He came to

Olivia and Radley's looking for me. He'll try to stop me from adopting Sami."

Cameron knew Alice had issues with her father, although she'd not confided much of her childhood. She didn't like to talk about it, and he hadn't pressed her. But even if her father was a bastard, Cameron didn't see how the man could influence the adoption process.

"I'm sure he was just trying to upset you."

"He did that all right." Her voice cracked as she suppressed tears.

"Sorry I wasn't there. Don't let him get to you." Cameron longed to hold her and provide moral support. He always missed her and Sami, always wished he was with them, but for the first time he felt frustrated and angry at the distance between them.

"Remember he's a judge in the family division of the High Court. He knows social workers in the adoption agencies."

Unease stole through Cameron. Was this man really in a position to influence the adoption process?

"Don't worry, love. Let me talk with Radley and Dad."

They moved on to happier topics. Alice told him what Sami had been doing that day.

"Love you, sweetheart," he said, and reluctantly ended the call.

In the distance came the familiar drone of a Chinook helicopter bringing in supplies to the nearby airfield under cover of dark.

Cameron tuned out the noise and stared at the lights of the refugee camp, his gaze losing focus. It sounded as though Radley had met Alice's father, and he was a pretty good judge of character. He called his brother to get an account of what had taken place.

"Olivia recognized him," Radley said. "She's never encountered him in court, thank goodness. He's got a grim reputation among the female lawyers. Sounds like he's a misogynist. I thought he seemed okay at first, but as soon as Alice turned up he started giving her a hard time. I didn't like him much."

"Did he really threaten to interfere in us adopting Sami?"

"I'm afraid so."

Cameron had hoped Alice was overreacting. "Perhaps I should resign from the army now and come home. Looks like I might end up having to do that anyway to satisfy the adoption requirements." He didn't like leaving Alice at home, worrying, facing all the anxiety and uncertainty alone.

"Call Dad first," Radley said. "Don't make any life-altering decisions until you've checked with him."

"Okay. Thanks, Rad."

Cameron tapped his phone on his knee, turning over what his brother had said. They had a problem with Alice's father by the sound of it. One more thing to overcome.

His phone vibrated against his knee and he glanced at the screen to see it was his father.

"Hello, Dad."

"Radley called me. Don't resign. I have a posting in the pipeline for you."

Cameron's dismal mood lightened at the enthusiasm in his father's voice. "I need some good news."

"This is a pet project of mine, something I've been pushing for. It's based in the UK and you'd be the perfect person to head it up. It would mean a promotion to lieutenant colonel if the idea works out."

A shiver of excitement passed through Cameron. He'd thought he'd be stuck at major for the rest of his career as he was considered a bit of a maverick. "Tell me more."

# Chapter Twelve

The black limousine slid through the rush hour traffic, the engine purring. Alice had never ridden in a limo before. She leaned back in the plush leather seat, enjoying the ride.

She had passed her driving test in time to pick Cameron up from the airport, but then everything changed. Three weeks before Christmas he was flying home early to take up a new post.

Cameron's father sat in the back with her, his attention absorbed by the documents on his lap. Every now and then he made a notation in the margin.

He had come straight from work in London and still wore his uniform, his hat laid on the seat between them. Alice felt underdressed in jeans, but she'd paired them with a pretty pink lacy cardigan. She had taken extra care with her makeup and straightened her hair so it hung down her back, sleek and shiny. Sami liked tangling his sticky fingers in her hair, so these days it was normally tied back.

Major General Knight put down his papers and glanced up. "Sorry to ignore you. I wanted to get this finished tonight."

She had grown used to him over the past weeks. He and Sandra sometimes babysat Sami. Cameron's father seemed less intimidating when he wasn't in uniform, but she still hadn't summoned the courage to call him George. She couldn't really call him by his military rank either, so she just avoided calling him anything. It was kind of embarrassing.

His phone chimed. Picking it up, he checked the screen. "Cameron's flight has landed on time."

Her excitement at seeing Cameron overcame her nerves. She bounced forward on the seat, staring out the window as they slowed to pass through the gates at RAF Brize Norton.

The limousine pulled up outside the terminal building. Major General Knight picked up his papers and straightened them. "You go on ahead and meet Cameron. I'll follow in a few minutes." He smiled, his eyes warm like Cameron's. Alice softened at the thought he was giving them time alone. Although he seemed a little scary at times, he was a kind man. She knew that from watching him play with Sami.

"Thanks." She pushed open the door and jumped out, then dashed through the airport entrance, heading for arrivals, her pulse racing.

She and Cameron had only been married for a short while, and half that time had been spent apart. Although they had talked nearly every day, it wasn't the same as being together. She couldn't wait to sink into his arms and kiss him again.

Cameron strode out through arrivals in his desert camouflage uniform, a bag slung over his shoulder. His hair was a little longer than when he left, and he was tanned a golden brown.

When he saw her, he dropped his bag and opened his arms. "Alice!"

Heart thumping, she ran towards him. He picked her up, swung her around, and kissed her.

"It's so good to be home," he whispered, his face buried against her neck. "I missed you so much."

He smelled of the desert, of dust and heat.

Memories rushed back of their days together in the field hospital. Even though her arm had been in a cast and she'd had nothing but the clothes on her back, those weeks were some of the best of her life.

"I missed you too."

He set her back on her feet but kept his arms around her, a grin on his face. "I wish you'd brought Sami. I can't wait to see him."

"Your dad said not to. Aren't we looking around your plane?"

"That's right. My new responsibility." Cameron kissed her again, then picked up his bag and gripped her hand. "Let's go and find my father."

Major General Knight stood a short distance away, a commanding figure, his hands linked behind his back.

"Dad!" Cameron embraced his father with obvious affection. The older man returned the hug with equal enthusiasm.

"You're looking fit and well, son. You certainly thrive in challenging conditions. This new posting should suit you perfectly. Are you looking forward to it?"

"You bet." Cameron looped his arm around Alice's waist.

Cameron had mentioned his new job would be based at Brize Norton and involved a plane, but that's all she knew. She'd been so excited at the thought of having him home with her and Sami, she hadn't asked for details.

They headed back to the limousine and climbed in while the driver stowed Cameron's bag.

"We need to go through a different gate to access the hangars," Major General Knight said.

Alice snuggled up to Cameron's side as the limo slid away, wishing they were alone so she could kiss him.

The car didn't travel far. They left the main terminal and took a private road to a military checkpoint. The tinted car window lowered and Cameron's father flashed his identification. They were quickly allowed through. The limousine followed the service road along the side of the runway towards a group of massive aircraft hangars at the far end of the compound.

Cameron and his dad chatted about the continuing conflict in Africa. Alice listened with half an ear, staring out the window. Lights gleamed in the gathering dusk through the fine misty rain. The car stopped outside the open door of a brightly lit hangar. A few people in army overalls were busy inside.

A massive dull green aircraft with a red cross on the side stood under the lights. The back was open, providing a ramp for them to walk up. Alice knew little about medical equipment, but one glance inside told her this was a mobile hospital.

"I thought you'd like to see where Cameron will be working," Major General Knight said to her. "Sandra tells me if she can picture where I am and what I'm doing, it helps her cope when I'm away."

"Thank you." He *was* thoughtful.

"Each deployment will be very short, though." Cameron squeezed her hand.

"A week at most," his father agreed. "On paper, your posting is here."

They halted in the belly of the plane. Beds, monitors, stretchers, oxygen cylinders, and other medical equipment she couldn't identify surrounded them.

Cameron released her hand and wandered about, opening metal units and checking everything out.

His father turned to Alice. "The RAF has units that specialize in providing role-one medical support for overseas operations. I've been pressing for the army to have its own deployable aeromedical teams for rapid response support in conflict zones. We need it for the initial few days before we establish a field hospital."

"So Cameron will take this mobile hospital oversees when a new war starts?"

"In a nutshell. It will also be scrambled for use in natural disasters and any occasion where we need a medical resource on the ground quickly."

"Sounds exciting." And dangerous, but no more so than working in a field hospital.

Cameron came back, smiling and nodding. "Excellent. The facilities are first class."

"You'll have a six-hour response time," his father said. "It'll require you to live nearby and be on standby."

"Not a problem. The rental property is close anyway. When we buy our own place, we'll search within a thirty-minute radius of the airport."

Taking her hand, Cameron led her around, showing her the equipment and explaining what some of it was used for. "What do you think, love?"

"It's wonderful. You get to live at home." She gave a little squeal and bounced on her toes to kiss him, bubbling with excitement at having him back.

"I get the best of both worlds, being with you and practicing my specialty where I'm most needed."

"And you're ideal for this position. It plays to all your strengths. You're good at motivating a team in challenging and dangerous conditions. Combine that with your experience in battlefield trauma and you are the perfect man to take control of this unit."

At his father's words, Cameron stood tall, eyes sparkling with excitement and pride. "Thanks for this opportunity, Dad. You really came through for me. I owe you one."

Cameron shook his father's hand and the two men embraced.

"You don't owe me anything, Cam. It's my pleasure."

Alice glowed inside to see her husband happy. This was a new start for them, one that should satisfy the social workers.

\*\*\*

Cameron climbed from the limo in front of his house. His mother ran out the front door with a cry of joy, threw her arms around his neck, and kissed his cheek. "My darling boy, it's so good to have you home. I breathe a sigh of relief every time one of my boys comes home safely, especially you. You're the reckless one."

"Not anymore, Mum. I have responsibilities now."

"That's good to hear."

His father passed him his bag and he carried it inside, Alice a few steps in front.

"Sami, look who it is. It's Daddy." Alice dropped to the floor behind Sami on his play mat and lifted the baby to sit between her legs.

Cameron couldn't believe how much his son had changed in the couple of months since he last saw him. He wore little denim dungarees, soft blue boots, and a matching T-shirt. His hair was longer as well. He gnawed on a bright pink and yellow toy in his hand.

Chest tight with emotion, Cameron dropped his bag and sank to his haunches. He'd missed so much of Sami's development. Would his little boy even recognize him?

"Hello, Samikins. Do you remember Daddy?"

His son dropped the toy and stretched out both arms towards Cameron, his lips parting in a happy smile, revealing two white teeth.

"Of course he recognizes you," his mother said.

With almost painful relief, Cameron scooped the child into his arms for a cuddle.

He kissed Sami's hair, then held him up above his head, jiggling him until he giggled. Drool trailed from the baby's mouth onto Cameron's shirt.

Alice jumped up and wiped it away with a cloth. "Poor baby is teething. You'll get used to the drool. There's a lot of it."

"Are my Samikins's toothies sore?"

Cameron's father cleared his throat from the

doorway. "Come on, Sandra. I think it's time we left these young people alone."

Cradling Sami in one arm, Cameron hugged and kissed his mother good-bye.

Alice gave his mother a kiss as well. "Sandra, thank you so much for babysitting Sami so I could see Cameron's hospital plane. It looks very exciting."

"You're welcome, dear. You know how much I love looking after my darling baby boy."

Cameron passed Sami to Alice, then followed his parents outside. "Thanks again, Dad." He embraced his father. He seemed to be doing a lot of hugging his dad today.

"Remember, you're meeting me in London tomorrow evening," his father said. "Sir Alistair Conway has a shock coming if he thinks he can interfere with my family."

"I'll come up on the train in the afternoon. I need to visit Hatton Garden and do some ring shopping."

His mother rested a hand on his shoulder and leaned close, her gaze moving to the door to check Alice wasn't listening. "Did you call the vicar?"

"Yep. The church is booked."

"Good. You'll have a busy week with the home visit from the adoption agency as well. But I'm sure that will be fine."

Cameron stepped back inside his house and closed the door as the limousine pulled away. He paused for a moment and smiled at the sound coming from upstairs—Alice chatting to Sami as she changed his diaper and the baby boy babbling back. It really was so good to be home with the two people he loved most in the world.

After his flight home, he should be tired and hungry. Yet all he hungered for was time with his family. He untied his boots, pulled them off, then grabbed his bag and ran upstairs, taking the steps two at a time.

Sami had moved into the second bedroom. Alice had transformed the room with blue and yellow walls and stenciled cartoon characters. She'd even assembled the flat-packed wooden crib on her own.

She'd discussed colors with him and sent him pictures of what she'd done, never making him feel guilty for not being here to help. She just got on with it. He gazed around, feeling like an outsider in her domain.

When they moved into their own place, he would make sure they decorated the nursery together and shared everything. He longed to be a full part of their lives.

"The room looks great, love."

"Thank you. I'm really pleased with how it turned out." She finished securing the closures on Sami's sleep suit and picked him up. "He just needs his bottle then we can pop him in bed. Do you want to feed him?"

"You do this feed. I'll take care of the next one. I need to jump in the shower." His skin was still sticky and gritty, and he longed to be clean.

A little while later Cameron emerged from the bathroom with a towel wrapped around his hips, and headed to his bedroom.

Alice lay on the bed in a silky blue nightdress, a plate of sandwiches and two glasses of wine on the nightstand. Cameron halted in the doorway, a grin pulling at his lips. It looked like his wife had the same idea he did. "Where's Sami?"

"In bed."

She rose and came to him, her sleek golden hair cascading over pale shoulders, her skin like polished ivory beneath the rich blue satin. How he had missed her, missed the gentle caress of her fingers, and the feel of her silky skin.

Heat seared along his veins, the weeks of wanting her coming back in a rush of almost uncontrollable longing.

She leaned in, her hair tickling his chest, and ran her fingertips over his pecs. "I thought we could have an early night. There are sandwiches if you're hungry."

"Sandwiches are the last thing on my mind." Cameron pulled her close, reveling in the feel of the woman he loved in his arms. He speared his fingers through her hair and cupped the back of her head as she stared up at him. "All I want right now is you."

He lowered his head and kissed her gently, enjoying the taste and feel of her soft mouth under his. Then he trailed his lips down her throat to the smooth skin of her shoulder. Her floral fragrance stoked the fire inside him, a fire he had tamped down and tried to forget while he was away. Now it roared nearly out of control as he slid his hands over his wife's delicate back and pulled her tightly against him.

Thank heavens for a home posting. He didn't want to be away from her again. Ever.


Cameron strode along St. James's Street towards Piccadilly, his father at his side. The streetlights cast bright streaks across the wet road. A black cab passed, followed by a red double-decker bus with a gruesome advertisement for the London Dungeon on the side.

He tapped a large manila envelope against his thigh as they waited to cross the road.

"You're sure this will work?" he asked.

"Absolutely," his father said.

They approached the neoclassical facade of the front of the club they were heading for and entered through a discreet black door.

The doorman met them. "Good evening, Major General Knight. It's a pleasure to see you, sir."

His father removed his hat and wedged it beneath his arm. Cameron followed suit. They had decided to wear their uniforms, anything to give them an edge.

"Can you tell me where Sir Alistair Conway is?" Cameron's father asked.

"I believe you'll find him in the library, sir."

"Thank you."

Cameron rarely entered the stuffy, old-fashioned club. His father spent time here every week, in the bastion of male power, networking. It meant on occasions like this, he had the contacts to get what he wanted.

They strode along the Victorian oak-paneled corridor to the hushed domain of politicians and civil servants. Groups of men dotted the room, seated in green leather chairs, relaxing with glasses of whiskey.

"That's our man." His father nodded to the far end of the room where a distinguished man in a dark suit sat reading the *Financial Times*.

Cameron swallowed hard as they threaded their way between the tables and chairs towards Alice's father. He had never met the man and didn't want to. But this had to be done. He would not lose Sami. He loved his baby boy, and Alice would be devastated if her father somehow kept them from adopting him.

Heart hammering with tension, he drew in a breath and steeled himself in much the same way he did before jumping out of a helicopter to tend a casualty.

They stopped near the man and his father cleared his throat. "Judge Conway?"

Alice's father looked up at the sound of his name. He stared at them for a moment, his gaze passing over the insignia of rank on their epaulets.

"I'm Major General Knight. I believe you met my eldest son the other day."

Alistair Conway's expression flashed from caution to alarm. "What can I do for you?" He rose to his feet, eyes narrowed suspiciously.

"I'm Major Cameron Knight." Cameron's voice came out gruff with nerves but he carried on, determined not to show weakness. "I'm your daughter's husband and Sami's dad."

The man frowned, his blue eyes like Alice's yet so different. There was no emotion in those eyes at all.

"I understand you don't want us to adopt Sami."

The man's gaze shot around the room, gauging whether anyone had heard. "Let's discuss this elsewhere."

Cameron held out the envelope. "That won't be necessary. This won't take long."

Alice's father stared at the envelope for a moment, then taking it, sat down and pulled the contents out on the table before him.

Cameron had hoped Conway's threats to interfere in Sami's adoption were nothing more than hot air, but according to his father, the judge was known to play dirty.

The man scanned the few sheets of paper. His gaze jumped back to them, eyes startled. "This happened at college. The three girls all retracted their allegations against me."

Major General Knight shrugged. "If the press gets a whiff of this, they'll send a reporter to find out the truth. Of course, if you didn't assault those women you have nothing to worry about."

"This is blackmail."

"No, this is defending my family. When Alice married Cameron she became a Knight. As far as I'm concerned, Sami is a Knight as well. The adoption paperwork is a mere formality."

Cameron's father bent and tapped a finger on the three incriminating sheets of paper he had acquired from the archives at Oxford University. "Do not interfere with my family, Judge Conway. You will not come out on top."

Cameron met the man's gaze and held his steady, following his father's example. After a few seconds,

Judge Conway looked away. Cameron turned and strode from the library at his father's side, victory and relief flaring in his chest.

# Chapter Thirteen

Alice held Sami up with his back against her chest so he could see the Christmas tree in the corner of Sandra and George's sitting room. Sami babbled, kicking his legs as if he wanted to get down and help decorate it.

Cameron, Radley, and little George hung brightly colored baubles on the branches of the tree while Olivia chased around the room after Emma, who had just begun walking. She kept picking decorations up and running away with them, giggling.

They had all gathered for a family dinner at Willow House, two weeks before Christmas, to celebrate the successful home visit the social workers had made to Alice and Cameron's place. The adoption agency had approved their home. Now Cameron was stationed in the UK for the next three years, they filled all the criteria to adopt. The only thing left was to make Sami's adoption legal in court. That would take place in a few months, when they could be fitted into the court schedule.

Cameron tickled Sami, making him squirm and giggle. "Do you like the Christmas tree, Samikins?"

"You do, don't you, sweetie." Alice cradled her son's diaper-padded bottom in her right hand and braced her left across his chest, still hoping Cameron might notice her bare third finger. He seemed oblivious to the absent wedding ring. She had resolved not to ask for one. She knew Cameron loved her. A ring was only a piece of metal.

He blew on Sami's tummy, then kissed Alice's hand, his gaze rising to hers as his lips touched her fingers. "What do you think about renewing our vows in the local church at Christmastime?"

"Renewing our vows? Isn't that something people do when they've been married for years?"

"The vicar says he can't marry us again. But if we renew our vows, we can have a ceremony in front of the family with the white dress, the flowers, and the cake. Would you like that?"

For a few seconds, Alice couldn't believe her ears.

"A proper wedding?"

"As good as." Cameron stroked back her hair, his eyebrows raised in question.

"Yes. Oh, yes." Excitement bubbled inside Alice. She leaned her cheek into Cameron's hand as he touched his lips to hers.

"I've been doing a little organizing on the sly." Sandra rested a hand on Alice's shoulder with a maternal smile. "My dear daughter-in-law, who's managed the seemingly impossible task of pulling my youngest son into line, deserves the best. The service will be short, but the vicar can fit you in on Christmas Eve."

Alice leaned into Cameron as he slipped his arm around her waist. He hadn't forgotten about her wedding ring after all. In fact, he'd done far more than simply buy a ring.

Sandra took Sami from Alice and stepped back while Cameron fished a blue velvet box from his pocket and flipped up the lid. "I thought you'd like something sparkly as well."

A beautiful sapphire and diamond ring winked at her in the firelight. She'd never owned expensive jewelry. Despite the fact her father was wealthy, she'd never owned anything much until recently.

Cameron lifted the ring out of the box and slipped it on her finger.

"It's lovely, Cam. Thank you." She threw her arms around his neck and kissed him, holding back, aware of the audience, when really she wanted to smother him in kisses. She'd have to do that later in private.

Sandra and Olivia crowded around to admire the ring. Cameron's father rose from his leather recliner by the French door where he'd been reading the newspaper and came to have a look. "Alice, I think it's about time you called me George. Or you can call me Dad, if you'd rather. I promise I don't bite."

Heat warmed her cheeks. She hadn't realized he'd noticed her awkwardness around him.

Sandra passed Sami back to her. She cuddled up against Cameron with her baby, so happy she almost burst with the feeling. "This will be the best Christmas ever."

"Ahh, Christmas." Olivia picked up a squirming Emma. "I love Christmas, especially in Sandra and George's house. It will always remind me of my first Christmas here six years ago, when Radley proposed to me."

"He proposed on Christmas Day?"

"At the dinner table."

"That's nearly as romantic as renewing our vows on Christmas Eve." She pressed a kiss to Cameron's cheek and he went back to decorating the tree.

"How did you meet Radley?"

"He came home on leave a week after I'd given birth. I needed so much help. I cringe to think how useless I was. I couldn't pick little George up for six weeks."

Alice opened her mouth, then closed it again, her brain processing. "You met Radley after George was born?" That didn't make sense.

An awkward silence fell over the room. Radley glanced at Cameron, who stared at the bauble in his hand. Olivia bit her lip, then busied herself wiping a smear off Emma's cheek. "No more Christmas chocolate for you, young lady. Not until Christmas Day."

She flashed an overly bright smile at Alice and headed for the door. "I need to check her diaper."

"I'll help you." Radley scooped a complaining George into his arms and headed after her. His parents followed.

The door closed behind them. The crackling log fire and the ticking clock were the only sounds left in the quiet room.

"What did I say?" she asked Cameron, glancing over her shoulder at the closed door.

Cameron dropped the bauble back in the box and ran a hand over his hair. "There's something I should have told you."

His somber tone flashed worry along her nerves. "You're scaring me, Cam."

"It's nothing to be scared about." He gave her a quick hug and guided her to the leather recliner that his father had vacated.

He sat on the chair opposite and rubbed his palms on his thighs. "Radley isn't George's father."

"Gosh. I had no idea. He looks so much like Radley."

"I know. That's because George is *my* son."

"Yours?"

Hot then cold flashed through Alice. George was Cameron's son. "How can that be?"

"Livi was my girlfriend in college. I got her pregnant by accident. It happens."

Alice just stared at him, her mind blank. A chill pervaded her chest, yet she had no urge to cry. All her emotions had been swept away, leaving her empty.

"You didn't want George?"

"Of course I did. I wanted to be his father." Cameron ran a hand over his mouth. "When Radley fell in love with Olivia, it got too complicated. I had to step back and let them be a family."

"So Radley adopted George?"

"Yes. He's officially George's father."

Alice struggled to draw breath through a throat clogged with a million questions, none of which she could vocalize. Cameron had given up the right to be George's father. Now he wanted to adopt Sami. She fought to pull the two things together and make them fit. Cameron was gentle and kind. He spent his whole career caring for people. The man she thought she knew would never have given up his son.

She closed her eyes and pressed her lips to Sami's soft hair, breathing in his reassuring baby smell. Cameron's fingers touched her hand. Instinctively she flinched away. She needed space.

"Give me a moment to get my head around this." Not only was George Cameron's son, it meant Olivia had been Cameron's lover. How did Radley cope with that? Surely he found it difficult.

She had been married to Cameron all these months, become part of the Knight family, yet he hadn't told her. None of them had. What must they have thought each time she commented how much George looked like Radley?

Alice pressed a hand over her eyes.

"I'm sorry, love. I didn't want to hurt you." His voice was thick with anguish.

"Why didn't you trust me enough to tell me sooner?"

"It wasn't that. I wanted to tell you before I went back to Africa. The time never seemed right. Then with all the hassle over the adoption, it went out of my mind."

She had to admit, the adoption worries had pretty much consumed her thoughts as well.

"This has nothing to do with you and me, or us and Sami. What happened between Olivia and me was years ago. We were students. I'm different now."

"You must be. I can't imagine you ever giving up your own son."

"If it had been anyone else but Radley marrying Olivia, I wouldn't have given up my rights to George. I didn't want to. It just seemed to be the right thing for him."

Alice's brain spun in circles, going over the same questions repeatedly, her raging emotions fogging her reason. "I need some time, Cam."

"Okay." He rose, hesitated at her side, then left the room without touching her, shutting the door softly behind him.

Sami wriggled and grunted, stretching his arms towards the door where his daddy had disappeared. Tears sprang into Alice's eyes. She hugged her little boy tightly and relaxed back in the chair. Breathing deeply, she tried to expel the tension so she could get her head around this.

Cameron had done what he thought was best for George. But how could he give up his own son? He loved George, that was obvious.

For what seemed like a long time, she sat and stared at the flickering flames of the log fire, letting her turbulent emotions settle until her normal common sense returned.

What he'd done in the past didn't matter. That was six years ago.

If she went back six years, she'd been a different person as well. She wouldn't have been ready to look after a baby back then, either.

What mattered was how Cameron behaved now, and he loved Sami.

She rose and carried her little boy out of the room, following the sound of muted voices to the kitchen.

Cameron sat at the large wooden kitchen table with his head in his hands, his mother at his side, her hand stroking his shoulder.

Sandra looked up as Alice came in, a tentative smile on her face.

"Sami is missing his daddy," Alice said, rounding the table to Cameron's side.

He glanced up, tears in his eyes. She had to swallow hard not to cry. He wrapped his arm around her and pulled her onto his lap, burying his face against her neck. Then he kissed her and Sami.

"Sorry," he mumbled.

"There's nothing to be sorry for." Alice framed his dear face in her hands and smiled at the man she loved so much, the man who had saved her life and given her a new life full of love and happiness.

She'd had nothing before she met Cameron, no loving family, no safe home. Now she had everything she could ever want.

He might have been irresponsible six years ago, but he wasn't any longer. The man she loved was a good man who cared for his family and spent his life saving the lives of soldiers. He was a man she was proud to call her husband. She couldn't wait to renew her wedding vows in front of his family.

The medieval church spire stood tall above the small stone cottages, silhouetted against a perfect blue winter's sky. Frosted tree branches framed the road and blinking Christmas lights shone from the villagers' tiny front gardens.

Alice gripped Cameron's hand and stared out the back window of Radley's 4x4 as it crunched along the icy road, circling the village green with its Christmas tree covered in sparkling color, to turn between the stone gateposts to the church car park.

The church bells pealed as family groups wrapped in

thick coats, hats, and scarves hurried out of the door after the Christmas Eve morning service. They jumped in their cars, eager to get out of the cold. Radley pulled close to the church door and cut the engine.

Although she and Cameron were already married, Alice's heart thudded with a mix of nerves and excitement. This time the ceremony was in front of their friends and family, in a proper church.

Cameron slipped an arm around her shoulders and kissed her cheek. "You ready, love?"

"I wonder if Mum and Dad are here." She leaned into him, resting her head on his lapel, listening to the steady beat of his heart. His lips pressed against her temple, then he dipped his head and found her mouth for a sweet kiss. A kiss that said whatever happened he was here for her, that he loved her, and nothing would change that. Even if her father tried to ruin their day.

"I shouldn't have invited them." But she had so badly wanted her mother here. She'd wanted her to come wedding-dress shopping with Sandra and Olivia as well. Her father had put a stop to that.

"If your father does anything to upset you, Dad will throw him out."

"Really?" Alice rarely saw anyone stand up to her father.

Cameron's gaze held hers and he nodded."Absolutely. I promise."

She smoothed her hand nervously across the skirt of her beautiful hand-beaded tulle wedding dress. Over the top she wore a white fur bolero shrug for warmth. Underneath, her legs were covered in white woolen tights decorated with sparkly stars. Once she saw the gorgeous dress, she was determined to find warm accessories so she could wear it in the winter.

Cameron climbed out and came around to open the door for her. Sandra, George and Olivia were already there with the children, waiting in their cars. Sandra and George had volunteered to look after Sami during the service. They got out when Alice did and loaded Sami in his stroller. Her baby boy was so handsome in his new green Christmas suit with tiny reindeer on his shirt and socks.

Emma was also strapped into her stroller. Olivia pushed her inside, closely followed by Radley with George in a stylish gray suit just like his father's.

Alice slipped her arm through Cameron's and trod carefully along the recently swept flagstone path to the church, taking the same route worshipers had walked to the old Norman building for nearly a thousand years.

It seemed strange entering a church for her wedding on the arm of her husband. From the start, nothing about her marriage had been normal.

The fragrance of pine, flowers, and beeswax polish welcomed her in through the arched portal. Wintery sunlight streamed in the stained-glass windows painting jewel-bright patterns of color along the aisle. A pretty nativity display sat to one side and holly and pine boughs trimmed with bows and baubles decorated the pew ends.

Alice gripped her bouquet of lilies nervously. Her gaze traveled over the people seated, waiting. The invitations had gone out at the last minute by e-mail. She hadn't expected many people to be free on Christmas Eve but many familiar faces were there.

Kelly Grace and Julia Braithwaite, both home on leave, smiled back at her. She hardly recognized the two women who had witnessed her wedding in Africa, both clad in dresses instead of dusty desert camouflage gear. Kelly Grace especially looked stunning with her red hair pinned up and some subtle makeup. No wonder Cameron had dated her.

Her dear friend Maeve had obviously managed to arrange cover for the women's refuge. She grinned and poked two thumbs in the air as Alice and Cameron walked past.

Most of the guests were Cameron's friends and relatives. A number of men in uniform stood among the civilian suits.

Although she smiled and nodded at people, part of Alice was focused on her father's neat dark hair at the front. She swallowed and tightened her grip on Cameron's arm. She shouldn't let her father get to her.

Alice's tension escalated as they neared the front of the church. Then little George stepped out from beside Radley and smiled up at her. "You look pretty, Auntie Alice."

He held out a lucky horseshoe on a ribbon. "Mummy says this makes you lucky."

"Will bring them luck," Olivia said in stage whisper.

Alice laughed, all her tension releasing. "Thank you very much." She slipped the ribbon over her wrist then stooped and kissed the little boy's cheek.

She'd forgotten George was to be Cameron's best man. He moved to Cameron's side, a serious smile on his face at the important part he was to play.

Cameron laid a hand proudly on the boy's shoulder. "Have you got the rings, bud?"

George opened his fist to display the two gold bands on his palm.

"Excellent. You hold on to those tightly until we need them."

Cameron grinned at Alice as they walked the last few steps and halted in front of the vicar.

After the short interruption, Alice's fears had fled. As they seemed to be breaking all the traditions, she reached out and hugged her mother. "I'm so pleased you're here," she whispered.

"I wouldn't have missed it. You look beautiful, darling." Her mother stepped back to her place, stunning in a lavender dress and matching hat.

Her father was stylish in a dark suit and high-collared shirt with a cravat. He nodded a greeting, and even managed a slight smile. He valued his public image too much to create a scene in front of Cameron's relatives. Today Alice could relax and enjoy herself.

The vicar welcomed everyone. "I'm very happy to see you here today, to bless the marriage of Cameron and Alice Knight, two young people who made their vows under trying circumstances. They now wish to restate their commitment to each other."

They sang a hymn and prayed. Then the vicar invited them to recall the vows they made at their wedding and they recited them again together.

When the time came, he asked George for the rings. The boy stepped forward solemnly and laid them on the vicar's book to be blessed. Cameron slipped a white gold band set with diamonds on the third finger of her left hand beside her engagement ring, and she put a plain gold band on his finger.

Her heart fluttered in her chest, so happy she couldn't stop grinning. Cameron lifted her hand and pressed his lips to it, his brown eyes twinkling with pleasure.

They kneeled to pray, and Alice thanked God for this wonderful man and his loving supportive family. She had wanted a wedding ring so much, but it was what it symbolized that mattered, Cameron's commitment to her and Sami.

When the vicar finally said they could kiss, she stood on her toes and threw her arms around Cameron's neck, not embarrassed to show everyone how much she loved this man. She was the luckiest woman in the world.

Cameron kissed her sweetly, then grasped her hand to lead her back down the aisle. Smiling faces greeted them as their friends and family approached to embrace her and slap Cameron on the back, wishing them luck.

A shiver of happiness ran through Alice, but her heart skipped a beat at the sound of her father's voice. He stepped forward and shook Cameron's hand. "You stand up for yourself. I like that."

He nodded to her and she did something she hadn't for a very long time, she rose on her toes and kissed her father's cheek. Today she was so happy she wanted to forgive, to wipe away the past and start afresh.

She could afford to be magnanimous. She was a Knight now, and the Knight family looked after their own. She and Sami would always be safe and loved. This Christmas would be the best ever and the start of the rest of her life.

# Author's Note

For those of you trying to work out where in Africa the story is set, I purposely kept it vague. As this story is set a little while in the future, I did not want to forecast conflict for any specific country.

The nomadic people mentioned are completely fictitious. I know of no nomadic African people who would reject a newborn baby because it has a cleft lip. This idea actually came from a documentary about the Ancient Greeks. Archeologists found a well in Athens full of babies' skeletons. Many of them had evidence of cleft palate, leading the researchers to believe these babies were killed because of this deformity.

The part of the story about babies and children with cleft lip and cleft palate not receiving the surgery they need is sadly true. In many parts of the world the people are too poor to afford this surgery, or the local medical provision is inadequate. If you were touched by Sami's plight, there is a wonderful charity called Operation Smile. Their volunteers travel the globe to provide life-altering surgery for those who have facial deformities. I'm sure they would welcome your support.

## The Army Doctor's Baby

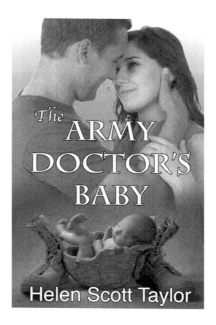

After his wife betrayed him, Major Radley Knight dedicated himself to becoming the best Army doctor he could be, dedicated himself to saving soldiers' lives. When he returns on leave from Afghanistan he is ready for a break. Instead he finds himself helping a young mother and her newborn baby. He falls in love with Olivia and her sweet baby boy and longs to spend the rest of his life caring for them. But Olivia and her baby belong to Radley's brother.

### *Praise for The Army Doctor's Baby*

"This is a sweet romance with a wonderful happily ever after. Highly recommend this read!" Luvbooks

"I loved this sweet, tender romance about a woman in need of a father for her baby and the man who falls in love with her..." Ruth Glick

"Loved the twists at the end of the book. Just the right amount of tension to keep me turning those pages! Totally recommend." Mary Leo

# About the Author

Helen Scott Taylor won the American Title IV contest in 2008. Her winning book, The Magic Knot, was published in 2009 to critical acclaim, received a starred review from *Booklist*, and was a *Booklist* top ten romance for 2009. Since then, she has published other novels, novellas, and short stories in both the UK and USA.

Helen lives in South West England near Plymouth in Devon between the windswept expanse of Dartmoor and the rocky Atlantic coast. As well as her wonderful long-suffering husband, she shares her home with a Westie a Shih Tzu and an aristocratic chocolate-shaded-silver-burmilla cat who rules the household with a velvet paw. She believes that deep within everyone, there's a little magic.

## Find Helen at:
http://www.HelenScottTaylor.com
http://twitter.com/helenscotttaylo
http://facebook.com/helenscotttaylor
www.facebook.com/HelenScottTaylorAuthor

# Book List

## Paranormal/Fantasy Romance

*The Magic Knot*
*The Phoenix Charm*
*The Ruby Kiss*
*The Feast of Beauty*
*Warriors of Ra*
*A Clockwork Fairytale*
*Ice Gods*
*Cursed Kiss*

## Contemporary Romance

*The Army Doctor's Baby*
*Unbreak My Heart*
*Oceans Between Us*
*Finally Home*
*A Family for Christmas*
*A Family Forever*
*Moments of Gold*
*Flowers on the water*

## Young Adult

*Wildwood*

Printed in Great Britain
by Amazon

75595542R00095